GULLIVER'S TRAVELS
to Lilliput and Brobdingnag

by
JONATHAN SWIFT

EDITED BY HUW PARKER

SERIES EDITOR: JOHN SEELY

BARRON'S

Acknowledgments

SWIFT, J.

The author and publishers are grateful to the following for permission to
reproduce illustrations and photographs:
Mansell Collection, pages 3 (bottom), 4, 6, 7.
Mary Evans Picture Library, pages 2, 3 (top).

Illustrated by Beverly Curl

First edition for the United States and Canada published 1999 by Barron's
Educational Series, Inc.

Thornes Classic Novels—Gulliver's Travels to Lilliput and Brobdingnag
By Jonathan Swift—Edited by Huw Parker
Series Editor—John Seely
Support Material © Huw Parker 1996
Original line illustrations © Stanley Thornes (Publishers) Ltd 1996
Gulliver's Travels first published in 1726
Thornes Classic Novels—Gulliver's Travels published in the UK in 1996 by:
Stanley Thornes (Publishers) Ltd
Ellenborough House, Wellington Street, Cheltenham G150 1YW

All inquiries should be addressed to:
Barron's Educational Series, Inc.
250 Wireless Boulevard
Hauppauge, New York 11788
http://www.barronseduc.com

Library of Congress Catalog Card No.: 99-25621
International Standard Book No. 0-7641-1149-3

Library of Congress Cataloging-in-Publication Data
Swift, Jonathan, 1667–1745.
    Gulliver's travels to Lilliput and Brobdingnag / by Jonathan Swift ;
edited by Huw Parker ; series editor, John Seely.
      p.   cm. — (Barron's classic novels)
    Summary: Chronicles an eighteenth-century Englishman's voyages
to such strange places as Lilliput, where people are six inches tall, and
Brobdingnag, a land peopled by giants. Includes explanatory notes
throughout the text, an introduction discussing the author and the back-
ground of the story, and a study guide.
    ISBN 0-7641-1149-3
    [1. Voyages and travels Fiction.   2. Fantasy].   I. Swift, Jonathan,
1667–1745.   Gulliver's travels.   II. Parker, Huw.   III. Title.   IV.
Series.
PZ7.S979Gu   1999
[Fic]—dc21
                                       99-25621
                                          CIP

Printed in the United States of America
987654321

DEC 1 4 2000

Contents

How to use this book

This edition of *Gulliver's Travels* is designed to help you get the most out of this story. It is presented in three parts:
- an introduction to the writer, the characters, and the setting of the story;
- the story itself;
- the study guide—questions to help you understand what you have read.

INTRODUCTION

This contains an illustrated introduction to the writer, the characters, and the setting of the story. You can read this material before starting the story, or you can leave it until later. If you get confused about people or places while reading the story, the introduction will make things clearer for you.

THE STORY

As well as the complete story itself, there are a number of other things to help you enjoy and understand it:
- at the beginning of each chapter, advice on what to look out for;
- on each page, a commentary that explains what is happening;
- on each page, notes that explain difficult words or expressions;
- "fast forward" and "rewind" sections (see below);
- illustrations of key moments;
- illustrations to help explain difficult words or expressions.

Fast forward/rewind sections

Some people like to read a story quickly to find out "what happens next," skipping the less important sections. If you like to do this, the sections you can jump are marked. A "fast forward" box (▶▶) tells you which page to jump to, a sign in the margin tells you where to start reading again, and a "rewind" box (◀◀) tells you what was on the pages you have skipped.

STUDY GUIDE

This contains advice and activities to use while you are reading the story and after you have finished it. There is a more detailed explanation of how to use it at the beginning of the study guide itself.

Introduction

ABOUT THE WRITER

Jonathan Swift was born in Dublin in 1667. His early years were difficult. His father died before he was born, and he spent the first three years of his life away from his mother with a nurse in Cumbria. When he returned to Ireland he grew up with little money, always dependent on others, and for the rest of his life he struggled to support himself.

Dublin in the eighteenth century

His Uncle Godwin looked after him until his own death in 1688. Swift then went to work for a family friend, Sir William Temple, in Surrey. Temple was a well-known and influential person, whose writing about issues of the time was widely read. During his time with Temple, two important things happened to Swift. First, he learned a lot about public life and became ambitious, believing that he had the ability to become a respected adviser to the highest people in the country. Secondly, he met a girl named Esther, whom he called "Stella." In 1695, when she was fifteen, he became her tutor and they developed an intense lifelong friendship.

Throughout his life he moved between Dublin and London, and in 1694 he was ordained a priest in Ireland and afterward began to spend more time there. (From 1713 he was the Dean of St. Patrick's Cathedral in Dublin.) When Sir William Temple died in 1699, Swift asked Stella to go over to Ireland, and she spent the remainder of her life there, always living near him. They constantly wrote to each other and Swift wrote a poem to celebrate each of her birthdays. Their relationship was strictly a friendship, which suited them both, but there is some evidence that they married secretly in 1716 in order to put off the attentions of another woman who was set on marrying Swift.

Throughout his life Swift wrote essays, pamphlets, poems, and books on issues of the time, such as the problems in Ireland. In his most famous essay, he attacked the injustices that led to starvation and poverty in Ireland by mimicking government officials and proposing that both problems would be solved by eating the children of the poor! His most important work was

Esther, Swift's lifelong friend, whom he called "Stella"

Gulliver's Travels, which was a huge success when it was published in 1726. One of Swift's friends wrote to him saying: "From the highest to the lowest it is universally read, from the cabinet-council to the nursery."

Swift died in 1745 after suffering from a tumor on the brain, which produced periods of deafness, blindness, and giddiness. During the last three years of his life he had suffered bouts of madness.

Jonathan Swift

THE SETTING

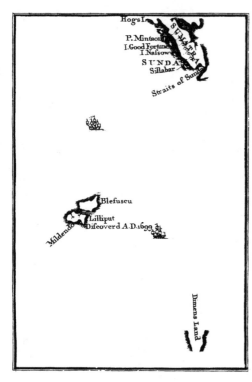

In the original version of *Gulliver's Travels*, Swift included the two maps printed here. These helped to give the impression that Lilliput and Brobdingnag actually existed. In fact, many people at the time were so taken in that they got out their atlases and tried to find them!

Map to show the location of Lilliput

Map to show the location of Brobdingnag

SIZES

Throughout *Gulliver's Travels*, Swift worked to specific measurements. It is helpful to bear these in mind when trying to picture the remarkable things that happen during the book. Basically, Swift used proportions of one to twelve. This was probably because he was working in feet and there are twelve inches to a foot, thus making calculations quite simple.

Therefore, when Gulliver is in Lilliput it is necessary to "shrink" everything to one-twelfth of its normal size. A Lilliputian adult is roughly six inches high (15 centimeters) —about the size of an ordinary pen.

When Gulliver is in Brobdingnag everything is twelve times larger than normal, so an adult there will be around 72 feet high (22 meters) —the height of four double-decker buses on top of each other!

Brobdingnagian

Gulliver

Lilliputian

GULLIVER'S OTHER TRAVELS

Swift created two other travels for Gulliver, which are not included in this book.

A Voyage to Laputa, Balnibarbi, Glubbdubdrib, Luggnagg, and Japan

After his voyage to Brobdingnag, Gulliver travels to a flying island called Laputa, which floats over a kingdom called Balnibarbi. Laputa is an exact circle with a diameter of four and half miles. The people who live on the island have their heads in the clouds—both in reality and in their obsession with ideas. Swift was attempting to laugh at the kind of people who are full of schemes and new ideas that are no practical use whatsoever. Their appearance gives them away. This is how Swift describes the Laputians:

> *Their heads were all reclined either to the right, or the left; one of their eyes turned inward, and the other directly up to the zenith.*

In other words, they are so busy gazing up at the clouds or daydreaming they are unaware of the real world around them. Because of this, many of them have servants whose job it is to guide them around the town so that they do not bump into everything in their way.

Laputa is in a very run-down state because the politicians talk about the latest theories or ideas but never actually do anything. Swift was drawing a parallel with English politicians, who he felt were full of fine words and grand promises, but never did anything about them.

Gulliver also has the opportunity to visit an island called Glubbdubdrib, which is a magical place where the spirits of famous people of the past can be summoned and talked to. Gulliver speaks to many historical figures and also to many famous people who had recently died. He learns through these discussions that the history of the human race is full of treachery, injustice, deceit, and corruption.

Swift's map of Laputa

A Voyage to the Country of the Houyhnhnms

Gulliver's final voyage is to a land ruled by horses called Houyhnhnms (the name sounding like a horse whinnying). These horses are different from those in England in that they have great intelligence and a language of their own. They have very high moral standards and discuss everything calmly and without prejudice. They live such pure lives that they have no word for "lying" and cannot understand what a war is.

Also living in this land is a race of creatures called Yahoos. They are a cross between apes and humans and are filthy and violent animals. They have no morals and are full of deceit and hatred, constantly fighting each other. When Gulliver arrives he is taken for a Yahoo, although he is not quite as hairy. The Houyhnhnms look down on the Yahoos and therefore also see Gulliver as inferior, though they accept that he has some intelligence.

Throughout his stay in their country Gulliver's admiration for the Houyhnhnms grows, as does his hatred for the Yahoos, who remind him of the worst aspects of human beings. Swift was trying to show, through this journey, what he thought were the worst aspects of people. He felt they often behaved like Yahoos, when they should try to become like Houyhnhnms. As in all the other travels, Swift's message is that human beings need to rid themselves of bad behavior and live good lives.

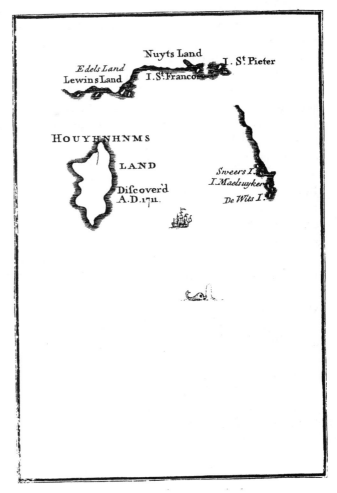

Swift's map of the land of Houyhnhnms

SATIRE AND *GULLIVER'S TRAVELS*

Swift was a satirical writer. Satirical writing aims to ridicule bad and foolish things in society. A modern example would be the skits on *Saturday Night Live* that attack the faults of famous people. Swift used the same techniques: He drew attention to the bad things that were happening in England through humor and exaggeration.

He had a lot of targets: politicians, lawyers, religious leaders, and military people to name but a few. The real target, however, was human nature. Swift said this about his work: "The chief end I propose in all my labours is to vex the world rather than divert it." His mission was not just to write an entertaining tale, but to provoke a reaction in people so that they would change their ways and become less tolerant of the injustices in society. His attack was on such human characteristics as hypocrisy (to say one thing but do another), vanity, envy, greed, lust, and the abuse of power. Throughout his travels Gulliver sees examples of all of these, and is forced into examining his own behavior.

The main technique that Swift used in *Gulliver's Travels* was the idea of size. At the end of Chapter 2 of the Voyage to Lilliput, Gulliver tells us that he has a "pocket perspective" (a telescope). This can be looked through at either end so that it enlarges or shrinks the object it is looking at. This is an image of the whole story. So when he is in Lilliput, human beings are seen as tiny, pathetic creatures who have an inflated view of themselves. Envy, jealousy, and political plotting are seen as petty and insignificant. The Lilliputians are, in reality, small-minded. Swift is therefore criticizing humans for their pride and arrogance in an attempt to bring us down to size!

In Brobdingnag we see human imperfections enlarged. Gulliver sees how ugly human skin is close up—even the most attractive Brobdingnagians look disfigured and unpleasant to Gulliver. Here Swift is claiming that when you examine human nature closely you discover many faults.

Although Swift is very critical of the human race, he cared very much about individuals:

> *I have ever hated all nations, professions, and communities, and all my love is towards individuals. For instance, I hate the tribe of lawyers, but I love Councillor Such-a-one and Judge Such-a-one . . . But principally I hate and detest that animal called man, although I heartily love John, Peter, Thomas and so forth.*

His satire was not aimed at individuals, but at groups of people who abused their position. He disliked the way in which people behave in a thoughtless and brutal manner.

PART ONE
A VOYAGE TO LILLIPUT

1

Look out for . . .
- the short biography of Gulliver's life leading up to his first journey. What do these details tell you about the kind of man he is?
- the way in which the Lilliputians and Gulliver react to each other.

The author giveth some account of himself and family; his first inducements to travel. He is shipwrecked, and swims for his life; gets safe on shoar in the country of Lilliput; is made a prisoner; and carried up the country.

My father had a small estate in Nottinghamshire; I was the third of five sons. He sent me to Emanuel College in Cambridge, at fourteen years old, where I resided three years, and applied myself close to my studies: but the charge of maintaining me (although I had a very scanty allowance) being too great for a narrow fortune; I was bound apprentice to Mr James Bates, an eminent surgeon in London, with whom I continued four years; and my father now and then sending me small sums of money, I laid them out in learning navigation, and other parts of the mathematics, useful to those who intend to travel, as I always believed it would be some time or other my fortune to do. When I left Mr Bates, I went down to my father; where, by the assistance of him and my uncle John, and some other relations, I got forty pounds, and a promise of thirty pounds a year to maintain me at Leyden: there I studied

maintaining me: supporting me financially
a narrow fortune: a lack of money
bound: made an
eminent: respected
navigation: the art of planning a journey for a ship
Leyden: a university in Holland renowned for medicine

COMMENTARY
Gulliver briefly describes his upbringing and early life during which he picks up skills in navigation and medicine. Both of these will be helpful to him during the course of his travels.

physic two years and seven months, knowing it would be useful in long voyages.

Soon after my return from Leyden, I was recommended by my good master Mr Bates, to be surgeon to the *Swallow*, Captain Abraham Pannell Commander; with whom I continued three years and a half, making a voyage or two into the Levant, and some other parts. When I came back, I resolved to settle in London, to which Mr Bates, my master, encouraged me; and by him I was recommended to several patients. I took part of a small house in the Old Jury; and being advised to alter my condition, I married Mrs Mary Burton, second daughter to Mr Edmond Burton, hosier, in Newgate Street, with whom I received four hundred pounds for a portion.

But my good master Bates dying in two years after, and I having few friends, my business began to fail; for my conscience would not suffer me to imitate the bad practice of too many among my brethren. Having therefore consulted with my wife, and some of my acquaintance, I determined to go again to sea. I was surgeon successively in two ships, and made several voyages, for six years, to the East and West Indies; by which I got some addition to my fortune. My hours of leisure I spent in reading the best authors, ancient and modern; being always provided with a good number of books; and when I was ashore, in observing the manners and dispositions of the people, as well as learning their language; wherein I had a great facility by the strength of my memory.

The last of these voyages not proving very fortunate, I grew weary of the sea, and intended to stay at home with my wife and family. I removed from the Old Jury to Fetter Lane, and from thence to Wapping, hoping to get business among the sailors; but it would not turn to account. After three years' expectation that things would mend, I accepted an advantageous offer from Captain William Prichard, Master of the *Antelope*, who was making a voyage to the South Sea. We set sail from Bristol, May 4th, 1699, and our voyage at first was very prosperous.

It would not be proper for some reasons to trouble the reader with the particulars of our adventures in those seas: let it suffice to inform him, that in

COMMENTARY

Gulliver marries and begins to practice medicine on the advise of his master, Mr. Bates. When Mr. Bates dies, Gulliver's business fails as he is too honest to cheat people. He therefore decides to travel as a ship's doctor, which gives him the opportunity to develop three hobbies: reading, observing other people's lifestyles, and learning languages.

physic: medicine
alter my condition: get married
hosier: a person who sells socks, stockings
suffer: allow
successively: one after another
dispositions: behavior
facility: skill
turn to account: become profitable
mend: improve
suffice: be enough

our passage from thence to the East Indies, we were driven by a violent storm to the north-west of Van Diemen's Land. By an observation, we found ourselves in the latitude of 30 degrees 2 minutes south. Twelve of our crew were dead by immoderate labour, and ill food; the rest were in a very weak condition. On the fifth of November, which was the beginning of summer in those parts, the weather being very hazy, the seamen spied a rock, within half a cable's length of the ship; but the wind was so strong, that we were driven directly upon it, and immediately split. Six of the crew, of whom I was one,

having let down the boat into the sea, made a shift to get clear of the ship, and the rock. We rowed by my computation, about three leagues, till we were able to work no longer, being already spent with labour while we were in the ship. We therefore trusted ourselves to the mercy of the waves; and in about half an hour the boat was overset by a sudden flurry from the north. What became of my companions in the boat, as well as of those who escaped on the rock, or were left in the vessel, I cannot tell; but conclude they were all lost. For my own part, I swam as fortune directed me, and was pushed forward by wind and tide. I often let my legs drop, and could feel no bottom: but when I was almost gone, and able to struggle no longer, I found myself within my depth; and by this time the storm was much abated. The declivity was so small, that I walked near a mile before I got to the shore, which I conjectured was about eight o'clock in the evening. I then advanced forward near half a mile, but could not discover any sign of houses or inhabitants; at least I was in so weak a condition, that I did not observe

---

Van Diemen's Land: Tasmania
immoderate: excessive
made a shift: made an attempt
computation: calculation
three leagues: nine miles (one league is about three miles)
spent with labour: exhausted
flurry: gust of wind
vessel: ship
declivity: slope
conjectured: guessed

COMMENTARY

The *Antelope* is wrecked in a storm. Although six sailors survive in the ship's boat, this too is wrecked by the storm and all the men, except Gulliver, drown. He manages to swim to land, showing both his ability to survive disaster and his tendency to have good luck when he needs it.

them. I was extremely tired, and with that, and the heat of the weather, and about half a pint of brandy that I drank as I left the ship, I found myself much inclined to sleep. I lay down on the grass, which was very short and soft; where I slept sounder than ever I remember to have done in my life, and as I reckoned, above nine hours; for when I awaked, it was just daylight. I attempted to rise, but was not able to stir: for as I happened to lie on my back, I found my arms and legs were strongly fastened on each side to the ground; and my hair, which was long and thick, tied down in the same manner. I likewise felt several slender ligatures across my body, from my armpits to my thighs. I could only look upwards; the sun began to grow hot, and the light offended mine eyes. I heard a confused noise about me, but in the posture I lay, could see nothing except the sky. In a little time I felt something alive moving on my left leg, which advancing gently forward over my breast, came almost up to my chin; when bending mine eyes downwards as much as I could, I perceived it to be a human creature not six inches high, with a bow and arrow in his hands, and a quiver at his back. In the meantime, I felt at least

COMMENTARY

Exhausted, Gulliver collapses and falls asleep. Waking up, he finds that he is fastened down by a lot of threads. Gulliver discovers that he has been tied down by a large number of small human creatures who are roughly twelve times smaller than him.

ligatures: ties
posture: position
perceived: understood

forty more of the same kind (as I conjectured) following the first. I was in the utmost astonishment, and roared so loud, that they all ran back in a fright; and some of them, as I was afterwards told, were hurt with the falls they got by leaping from my sides upon the ground. However, they soon returned; and one of them, who ventured so far as to get a full sight of my face, lifting up his hands and eyes by way of admiration, cried out in a shrill, but distinct voice, *Hekinah degul*: the others repeated the same words several times, but I then knew not what they meant. I lay all this while, as the reader may believe, in great uneasiness: at length, struggling to get loose, I had the fortune to break the strings, and wrench out the pegs that fastened my left arm to the ground; for, by lifting it up to my face, I discovered the methods they had taken to bind me; and, at the same time, with a violent pull, which gave me excessive pain, I a little loosened the strings that tied down my hair on the left side; so that I was just able to turn my head about two inches. But the creatures ran off a second time, before I could seize them; whereupon there was a great shout in a very shrill accent; and after it ceased, I heard one of them cry aloud, *Tolgo phonac*; when in an instant I felt above an hundred arrows discharged on my left hand, which pricked me like so many needles; and besides, they shot another flight into the air, as we do bombs in Europe; whereof many, I suppose, fell on my body (though I felt them not), and some on my face, which I immediately covered with my left hand. When this shower of arrows was over, I fell a groaning with grief and pain; and then striving again to get loose, they discharged another volley larger than the first; and some of them attempted with spears to stick me in the sides; but, by good luck, I had on me a buff jerkin, which they could not pierce. I thought it the most prudent method to lie still; and my design was to continue so till night, when my left hand being already loose, I could easily free myself: and as for the inhabitants, I had reason to believe I might be a match for the greatest armies they could bring against me, if they were all of the same size with him that I saw. But fortune disposed otherwise of me. When the people observed I was quiet, they discharged no more arrows: but by the noise increasing, I knew their numbers

ventured: dared come
discharged: fired
buff jerkin: leather vest
prudent: wise
design: plan
disposed otherwise of me: had different
  ideas for me

COMMENTARY
When Gulliver shouts out the creatures are so terrified they run off, though they soon return. When he eventually frees his left arm, the little people are so terrified they start firing arrows at him and stabbing him with their tiny spears. Because Gulliver is wearing thick clothing, the arrows and spears do not hurt him much. He plans to escape later that night, as he feels he could easily overpower these little people.

were greater; and about four yards from me, over-against my right ear, I heard a knocking for above an hour, like people at work; when turning my head that way, as well as the pegs and strings would permit me, I saw a stage erected about a foot and half from the ground, capable of holding four of the inhabitants, with two or three ladders to mount it: from whence one of them, who seemed to be a person of quality, made me a long speech, whereof I understood not one syllable. But I should have mentioned, that before the principal person began his oration, he cried out three times *Langro dehul san* (these words and the former were afterwards repeated and explained to me): whereupon immediately about fifty of the inhabitants came, and cut the strings that fastened the left side of my head, which gave me the liberty of turning it to the right, and of observing the person and gesture of him who was to speak. He appeared to be of a middle age, and taller than any of the other three who attended him; whereof one was a page, who held up his train, and seemed to be somewhat longer than my middle finger; the other two stood one on each side to support him. He acted every part of an orator; and I could observe many periods of threatenings, and others of promises, pity and kindness. I answered in a few words, but in the most submissive manner, lifting up my left hand and both mine eyes to the sun, as calling him for a witness; and being almost famished with hunger, having not eaten a morsel for some hours before I left the ship, I found the demands of nature so strong upon me that I could not forbear showing my impatience (perhaps against the strict rules of decency) by putting my finger frequently on my mouth, to signify that I wanted food. The *Hurgo* (for so they call a great lord, as I afterwards learnt) understood me very well: he descended from the stage, and commanded that several ladders should be applied to my sides, on which above an hundred of the inhabitants mounted, and walked towards my mouth, laden with baskets full of meat, which had been provided, and sent thither by the King's orders upon the first intelligence he received of me. I observed there was the flesh of several animals, but could not distinguish them by the taste. There were shoulders, legs, and loins shaped like those of mutton, and very

COMMENTARY

Gulliver notices that the little people have built a platform near his head upon which one of their leaders is standing. He and Gulliver have to communicate through gestures as they speak different languages. Gulliver feels very hungry and indicates that he would like food. The Lilliputians have already prepared for this, which indicates that they do not intend to kill Gulliver but have plans for him.

a person of quality: an important person
oration: speech
page: personal servant
orator: skilled speaker
submissive: pleading
famished: starving
morsel: scrap of food
forbear: help
decency: good manners
thither: there
intelligence: news

well dressed, but smaller than the wings of a lark. I eat them by two or three at
a mouthful, and took three loaves at a time, about the bigness of musket
bullets. They supplied me as fast as they could, showing a thousand marks of
wonder and astonishment at my bulk and appetite. I then made another sign
that I wanted drink. They found by my eating that a small quantity would not
suffice me; and being a most ingenious people, they slung up with great
dexterity one of their largest hogsheads; then rolled it towards my hand, and
beat out the top; I drank it off at a draught, which I might well do, for it
hardly held half a pint, and tasted like a small wine of burgundy, but much
more delicious. They brought me a second hogshead, which I drank in the
same manner, and made signs for more, but they had none to give me. When I
had performed these wonders, they shouted for joy, and danced upon my
breast, repeating several times as they did at first, *Hekinah degul*. They made me
a sign that I should throw down the two hogsheads, but first warned the
people below to stand out of the way, crying aloud, *Borach mivola*; and when
they saw the vessels in the air, there was an universal shout of *Hekinah degul*. I
confess I was often tempted, while they were passing backwards and forwards
on my body, to seize forty or fifty of the first that came in my reach, and dash
them against the ground. But the remembrance of what I had felt, which
probably might not be the worst they could do; and the promise of honour I
made them, for so I interpreted my submissive behavior, soon drove out
those imaginations. Besides, I now considered myself as bound by the laws of
hospitality to a people who had treated me with so much expence and
magnificence. However, in my thoughts I could not sufficiently wonder at the
intrepidity of these diminutive mortals, who durst venture to mount and
walk on my body, while one of my hands was at liberty, without trembling at
the very sight of so prodigious a creature as I must appear to them. After some
time, when they observed that I made no more demands for meat, there
appeared before me a person of high rank from his imperial majesty. His
excellency having mounted on the small of my right leg, advanced forwards up
to my face, with about a dozen of his retinue. And producing his credentials

musket: rifle
dexterity: skill
hogsheads: barrels
at a draught: chugalugging
sufficiently wonder:
   wonder enough
intrepidity: courage
diminutive: tiny
durst: dared
at liberty: free
prodigious: huge
retinue: followers
credentials: letters
   showing his importance

COMMENTARY
Because of the difference in size, the little people have to give Gulliver baskets full of meat and bread and barrels of wine to satisfy him. Gulliver thinks again about escaping, this time by grabbing some of the Lilliputians and killing them. However, he decides that they have been kind to him and that he should be grateful.

under the signet royal, which he applied close to mine eyes, spoke about ten minutes, without any signs of anger, but with a kind of determinate resolution; often pointing forwards, which, as I afterwards found was towards the capital city, about half a mile distant, whither it was agreed by his majesty in council that I must be conveyed. I answered in few words, but to no purpose, and made a sign with my hand that was loose, putting it to the other (but over his excellency's head, for fear of hurting him or his train) and then to my own head and body, to signify that I desired my liberty. It appeared that he understood me well enough; for he shook his head by way of disapprobation, and held his hand in a posture to show that I must be carried as a prisoner. However, he made other signs to let me understand that I should have meat and drink enough, and very good treatment. Whereupon I once more thought of attempting to break my bonds; but again, when I felt the smart of their arrows upon my face and hands, which were all in blisters, and many of the darts still sticking in them; and observing likewise that the number of my enemies encreased; I gave tokens to let them know that they might do with me what they pleased. Upon this, the *Hurgo* and his train withdrew, with much civility and chearful countenances. Soon after I heard a general shout, with frequent repetitions of the words, *Peplom selan*, and I felt great numbers of the people on my left side relaxing the cords to such a degree, that I was able to turn upon my right, and to ease myself with making water; which I very plentifully did, to the great astonishment of the people, who conjecturing by my motions what I was going to do, immediately opened to the right and left on that side, to avoid the torrent which fell with such noise and violence from me. But before this, they had daubed my face and both my hands with a sort of ointment very pleasant to the smell, which in a few minutes removed all the smart of their arrows. These circumstances, added to the refreshment I had received by their victuals and drink, which were very nourishing, disposed me to sleep. I slept about eight hours as I was afterwards assured; and it was no wonder; for the physicians, by the Emperor's order, had mingled a sleeping potion in the hogsheads of wine.

COMMENTARY

Gulliver and the person of high rank communicate through gestures. Gulliver learns that he will be taken to the city and cannot be released yet. Again Gulliver thinks of escaping, but this time is put off by the thought of the pain caused by the arrows and spears. The wounds already caused are soothed by an ointment that the Lilliputians put on him. Having drunk so much, Gulliver feels an urgent need to relieve himself and, turning over, urinates on the ground. This appears like a great flood to the Lilliputians who quickly get out of the way. (Throughout the book Gulliver often refers to bodily functions.)

signet royal: royal stamp
determinate resolution: clear confidence
conveyed: taken
disapprobation: disapproval
tokens: signs
civility: politeness
countenances: faces
making water: urinating
torrent: flood
daubed: spread
victuals: food
physicians: doctors

It seemed that upon the first moment I was discovered sleeping on the ground after my landing, the Emperor had early notice of it by an express; and determined in council that I should be tied in the manner I have related (which was done in the night while I slept), that plenty of meat and drink should be sent to me, and a machine prepared to carry me to the capital city.

This resolution perhaps may appear very bold and dangerous, and I am confident would not be imitated by any prince in Europe on the like occasion; however, in my opinion it was extremely prudent as well as generous. For supposing these people had endeavoured to kill me with their spears and arrows while I was asleep; I should certainly have awaked with the first sense of smart, which might so far have roused my rage and strength, as to enable me to break the strings wherewith I was tied; after which, as they were not able to make resistance, so they could expect no mercy.

These people are most excellent mathematicians, and arrived to a great perfection in mechanics by the countenance and encouragement of the Emperor, who is a renowned patron of learning. This prince hath several machines fixed on wheels for the carriage of trees and other great weights. He often buildeth his largest men of war, whereof some are nine foot long, in the woods where the timber grows, and has them carried on these engines three or four hundred yards to the sea. Five hundred carpenters and engineers were immediately set at work to prepare the greatest engine they had. It was a frame of wood raised three inches from the ground, about seven foot long and four wide, moving upon twenty two wheels. The shout I heard, was upon the arrival of this engine, which, it seems, set out in four hours after my landing. It was brought parallel to me as I lay. But the principal difficulty was to raise and place me in this vehicle. Eighty poles, each of one foot high, were erected for this purpose, and very strong cords of the bigness of packthread were fastened by hooks to many bandages, which the workmen had girt round my neck, my hands, my body, and my legs. Nine hundred of the strongest men were employed to draw up these cords by many pullies fastened on the poles, and thus in less than three hours, I was raised and slung into the engine, and there

---

express: message
resolution: decision
the like: a similar
endeavoured: attempted
countenance: support
patron: supporter
men of war: battleships
packthread: strong sewing thread
girt: encircled

COMMENTARY
The Lilliputians, whom Gulliver describes as excellent mechanics, build a large machine to carry Gulliver, asleep, to the city.

tied fast. All this I was told; for while the whole operation was performing, I lay in a profound sleep, by the force of that soporiferous medicine infused into my liquor. Fifteen hundred of the Emperor's largest horses, each about four inches and a half high, were employed to draw me towards the metropolis, which, as I said, was a mile distant.

About four hours after we began our journey, I awaked by a very ridiculous accident; for the carriage being stopt a while to adjust something that was out of order, two or three of the young natives had the curiosity to see how I looked when I was asleep; they climbed up into the engine, and advancing very softly to my face, one of them, an officer in the guards, put the sharp end of his half-pike a good way up into my left nostril, which tickled my nose like a straw, and made me sneeze violently: whereupon they stole off unperceived; and it was three weeks before I knew the cause of my awaking so suddenly. We made a long march the remaining part of the day, and rested at night with five hundred guards on each side of me, half with torches, and half with bows and arrows, ready to shoot me if I should offer to stir. The next morning at sunrise we continued our march, and arrived within two hundred yards of the city gates about noon. The Emperor, and all his court, came out to meet us; but his great officers would by no means suffer his majesty to endanger his person by mounting on my body.

At the place where the carriage stopped, there stood an ancient temple, esteemed to be the largest in the whole kingdom; which having been polluted some years before by an unnatural murder, was, according to the zeal of those people, looked upon as profane, and therefore had been applied to common use, and all the ornaments and furniture carried away. In this edifice it was determined I should lodge. The great gate fronting to the north was about four foot high, and almost two foot wide, through which I could easily creep. On each side of the gate was a small window not above six inches from the ground: into that on the left side, the king's smiths conveyed fourscore and eleven chains, like those that hang to a lady's watch in Europe, and almost as large, which were locked to my left leg with six and thirty padlocks. Over

COMMENTARY

On his way to the city, Gulliver is awakened by a curious soldier putting a spear up his nose, causing him to sneeze. The emperor meets Gulliver on his arrival at the city. Gulliver is chained to a disused temple, which is the largest one in Lilliput, though it is just big enough for Gulliver to lie down in.

soporiferous: sleep-inducing
infused: put
metropolis: city
half-pike: spear
unperceived: unnoticed
zeal: religious enthusiasm
profane: useless for religious activities
edifice: building
smiths: blacksmiths
fourscore: eighty

against this temple, on the other side of the great highway, at twenty foot distance, there was a turret at least five foot high. Here the Emperor ascended with many principal lords of his court, to have an opportunity of viewing me, as I was told, for I could not see them. It was reckoned that above an hundred thousand inhabitants came out of the town upon the same errand; and in spite of my guards, I believe there could not be fewer than ten thousand, at several times, who mounted upon my body by the help of ladders. But a proclamation was soon issued to forbid it, upon pain of death. When the workmen found it was impossible for me to break loose, they cut all the strings that bound me; whereupon I rose up with as melancholy a disposition as ever I had in my life. But the noise and astonishment of the people at seeing me rise and walk, are not to be expressed. The chains that held my left leg were about two yards long, and gave me not only the liberty of walking backwards and forwards in a semicircle; but being fixed within four inches of the gate, allowed me to creep in, and lie at my full length in the temple.

errand: *business*
proclamation: official announcement
melancholy: sad
disposition: mood

COMMENTARY

The people are so curious to see Gulliver that vast crowds numbering one hundred thousand turn out to stare at him and clamber on him. However, a law is made to ban people from doing this. When Gulliver is freed from all the strings (though still chained to the temple by his left leg), he stands up and the people are once more astonished by his size.

2

Look out for . . .
- the personality of the emperor. How much trust is there between him and Gulliver?
- the Lilliputians' description of Gulliver's belongings. Why do you think Swift describes the objects like this rather than just telling us what they are?

The Emperor of Lilliput, attended by several of the nobility, comes to see the author in his confinement. The Emperor's person and habit described. Learned men appointed to teach the author their language. He gains favour by his mild disposition. His pockets are searched, and his sword and pistols taken from him.

When I found myself on my feet, I looked about me, and must confess I never beheld a more entertaining prospect. The country round appeared like a continued garden; and the inclosed fields, which were generally forty foot square, resembled so many beds of flowers. These fields were intermingled with woods of half a stang, and the tallest trees, as I could judge, appeared to be seven foot high. I viewed the town on my left hand, which looked like the painted scene of a city in a theatre.

I had been for some hours extremely pressed by the necessities of nature; which was no wonder, it being almost two days since I had last disburthened myself. I was under great difficulties between urgency and shame. The best expedient I could think on, was to creep into my house, which I accordingly

COMMENTARY
When Gulliver gets to his feet, he looks around and is amazed at how small everything is. Gulliver urgently needs to go to the bathroom but is embarrassed, so he steps back into his house and relieves himself there.

confinement: imprisonment
habit: clothing
prospect: view
intermingled: mixed in
stang: short pole
necessities of nature: need to go to the bathroom
disburthened: relieved
expedient: plan

did; and shutting the gate after me, I went as far as the length of my chain would suffer; and discharged my body of that uneasy load. But this was the only time I was ever guilty of so uncleanly an action; for which I cannot but hope the candid reader will give some allowance, after he hath maturely and impartially considered my case, and the distress I was in. From this time my constant practice was, as soon as I rose, to perform that business in open air, at the full extent of my chain; and due care was taken every morning before company came, that the offensive matter should be carried off in wheel-barrows, by two servants appointed for that purpose. I would not have dwelt so long upon a circumstance, that perhaps at first sight may appear not very momentous; if I had not thought it necessary to justify my character in point of cleanliness to the world; which I am told, some of my maligners have been pleased, upon this and other occasions, to call in question.

When this adventure was at an end, I came back out of my house, having occasion for fresh air. The Emperor was already descended from the tower, and advancing on horseback toward me, which had like to have cost him dear; for the beast, although very well trained, yet wholly unused to such a sight, which appeared as if a mountain moved before him, reared up on his hinder feet: but that prince, who is an excellent horseman, kept his seat, until his attendants ran in, and held the bridle, while his majesty had time to dismount. When he alighted, he surveyed me round with great admiration, but kept beyond the length of my chains. He ordered his cooks and butlers, who were already prepared, to give me victuals and drink, which they pushed forward in a sort of vehicles upon wheels until I could reach them. I took those vehicles, and soon emptied them all; twenty of them were filled with meat, and ten with liquor; each of the former afforded me two or three good mouthfuls, and I emptied the liquor of ten vessels, which was contained in earthen vials, into one vehicle, drinking it off at a draught; and so I did with the rest. The Empress, and young princes of the blood, of both sexes, attended by many ladies, sat at some distance in their chairs; but upon the accident that happened to the Emperor's horse, they alighted, and came near his person; which I am now

discharged: relieved
candid: unbiased
impartially: without prejudice
circumstance: situation
momentous: important
maligners: slanderers
vessels: cups
vials: bottles

COMMENTARY
Gulliver tells us that on future occasions servants came with wheelbarrows to clear away his excrement. He is very concerned that readers understand the difficult position he was in and do not think badly of him. Following this, the emperor and members of his court visit and Gulliver is provided with more food and drink.

going to describe. He is taller by almost the breadth of my nail, than any of his court; which alone is enough to strike an awe into the beholders. His features are strong and masculine, with an Austrian lip, and arched nose, his complexion olive, his countenance erect, his body and limbs well proportioned, all his motions graceful, and his deportment majestic. He was then past his prime, being twenty-eight years and three quarters old, of which he had reigned about seven, in great felicity, and generally victorious. For the better convenience of beholding him, I lay on my side, so that my face was parallel to his, and he stood but three

yards off: however, I have had him since many times in my hand, and therefore cannot be deceived in the description. His dress was very plain and simple, the fashion of it between the Asiatic and the European; but he had on his head a light helmet of gold, adorned with jewels, and a plume on the crest. He held his sword drawn in his hand, to defend himself, if I should happen to break loose; it was almost three inches long, the hilt and scabbard were gold enriched with diamonds. His voice was shrill, but very clear and articulate, and I could distinctly hear it when I stood up. The ladies and courtiers were all most magnificently

COMMENTARY

The emperor is described. He is the tallest member of the court, and in clothing and looks he is quite majestic. In fact, all the members of the court are dressed magnificently.

an awe: respect
Austrian lip: Swift is perhaps mocking
    George I who was of Germanic origin
countenance erect: upright appearance
deportment: way of carrying himself
in great felicity: with great skill
articulate: easy to understand
distinctly: clearly
courtiers: members of the court

clad, so that the spot they stood upon seemed to resemble a petticoat spread on the ground, embroidered with figures of gold and silver. His imperial majesty spoke often to me, and I returned answers, but neither of us could understand a syllable. There were several of his priests and lawyers present (as I conjectured by their habits) who were commanded to address themselves to me, and I spoke to them in as many languages as I had the least smattering of, which were high and low Dutch, Latin, French, Spanish, Italian, and Lingua Franca; but all to no purpose. After about two hours the court retired, and I was left with a strong guard, to prevent the impertinence, and probably the malice of the rabble, who were very impatient to crowd about me as near as they durst; and some of them had the impudence to shoot their arrows at me as I sat on the ground by the door of my house; whereof one very narrowly missed my left eye. But the colonel ordered six of the ringleaders to be seized, and thought no punishment so proper as to deliver them bound into my hands, which some of his soldiers accordingly did, pushing them forwards with the butt-ends of the pikes into my reach: I took them all in my right hand, put five of them into my coat-pocket; and as to the sixth, I made a countenance as if I would eat him alive. The poor man squalled terribly, and the colonel and his officers were in much pain, especially when they saw me take out my penknife: but I soon put them out of fear; for, looking mildly, and immediately cutting the strings he was bound with, I set him gently on the ground, and away he ran. I treated the rest in the same manner, taking them one by one out of my pocket; and I observed, both the soldiers and people were highly obliged at this mark of my clemency, which was represented very much to my advantage at court.

Towards night I got with some difficulty into my house, where I lay on the ground, and continued to do so about a fortnight; during which time the Emperor gave orders to have a bed prepared for me. Six hundred beds of the common measure were brought in carriages, and worked up in my house; an hundred and fifty of their beds sewn together made up the breadth and length, and these were four double, which however kept me but very indifferently

high and low Dutch:
German and Dutch
Lingua Franca:
a made-up language
countenance: face
squalled: wailed
highly obliged: very
pleased
clemency: mercy
common measure:
usual size
but very indifferently:
only a little

COMMENTARY
The emperor tries unsuccessfully to communicate with Gulliver, even though Gulliver tries out all the languages he knows. After the emperor leaves, some of the crowd get restless and a few even fire arrows at Gulliver. The ringleaders are arrested and given to Gulliver to punish. He pretends to eat them but then shows mercy and releases them. This earns him the respect of the people.

from the hardness of the floor, that was of smooth stone. By the same computation they proved me with sheets, blankets and coverlets, tolerable enough for one who had been so long enured to hardships as I.

As the news of my arrival spread through the kingdom, it brought prodigious numbers of rich, idle, and curious people to see me; so that the villages were almost emptied, and great neglect of tillage and household affairs must have ensued, if his imperial majesty had not provided by several proclamations and orders of state against this inconveniency. He directed that those, who had already beheld me, should return home, and not presume to come within fifty yards of my house, without licence from court; whereby the secretaries of state got considerable fees.

In the meantime, the Emperor held frequent councils to debate what course should be taken with me; and I was afterwards assured by a particular friend, a person of great quality, who was much in the secret as any; that the court was under many difficulties concerning me. They apprehended my breaking loose; that my diet would be very expensive, and might cause a famine. Sometimes they determined to starve me, or at least to shoot me in the face and hands with poisoned arrows, which would soon dispatch me: but again they considered, that the stench of so large a carcase might produce a plague in the metropolis, and probably spread through the whole kingdom. In the midst of these consultations, several officers of the army went to the door of the great council-chamber; and two of them being admitted, gave an account of my behaviour to the six criminals abovementioned; which made so favourable an impression in the breast of his majesty, and the whole board, in my behalf, that an imperial commission was issued out, obliging all the villages nine hundred yards round the city to deliver in every morning six beeves, forty sheep, and other victuals for my sustenance; together with a proportionable quantity of bread and wine, and other liquors: for the due payment of which his majesty gave assignments upon his treasury. For this prince lives chiefly upon his own demesnes; seldom, except upon great occasions raising any subsidies upon his subjects, who are bound to attend him in his wars at their own expence. An

COMMENTARY

The emperor makes a law that bans people from coming to see Gulliver more than once, as it is affecting their work. Meanwhile, Gulliver's future is debated at court. Some are worried that he is going to eat too much of the country's food and they suggest starving or poisoning him. However, the news of Gulliver's merciful act settles the emperor's mind, and he orders that everybody in the kingdom should contribute toward feeding Gulliver.

tolerable: bearable
tillage: cultivation
apprehended: worried about
dispatch: get rid of
imperial commission: royal order
beeves: cattle
proportionable: equal
gave assignments upon: paid out of
demesnes: wealth and land
subsidies: taxes

establishment was also made of six hundred persons to be my domestics, who
had board-wages allowed for their maintenance, and tents built for them very
conveniently on each side of my door. It was likewise ordered, that three
hundred taylors should make me a suit of clothes after the fashion of the
country: that, six of his majesty's greatest scholars should be employed to
instruct me in their language: and, lastly, that the Emperor's horses, and those
of the nobility, and troops of guards, should be exercised in my sight, to
accustom themselves to me. All these orders were duly put in execution; and in
about three weeks I made a great progress in learning their language; during
which time, the Emperor frequently honoured me with his visits, and was
pleased to assist my masters in teaching me. We began already to converse
together in some sort; and the first words I learnt, were to express my desire,
that he would please to give me my liberty; which I every day repeated on my
knees. His answer, as I could apprehend, was, that this must be a work of time,
not to be thought on without the advice of his council; and that first I must
lumos kelmin pesso desmar lon emposo; that is, *swear a peace with him and his kingdom.*

However, that I should be used with all
kindness; and he advised me to acquire
by my patience and discreet behaviour,
the good opinion of himself and his
subjects. He desired I would not take
ill, if he gave orders to certain proper
officers to search me; for probably I
might carry about me several weapons,
which must needs be dangerous things,
if they answered the bulk of so
prodigious a person. I said, his majesty
should be satisfied, for I was ready to
strip myself, and turn up my pockets
before him. This I delivered, part in
words and part in signs. He replied,

establishment: provision
domestics: servants
board-wages: money paid to provide them
   with food to live on
apprehend: understand
discreet: tactful

COMMENTARY
Gulliver is provided with servants,
clothing (made especially for him), and
teachers who help him to learn the
Lilliputian language. The emperor often
visits him, and Gulliver continually asks
to be released but is told to be patient.
The emperor also asks for Gulliver's
permission to carry out a search of his
clothing.

that by the laws of the kingdom, I must be searched by two of his officers: that he knew this could not be done without my consent and assistance, that he had so good an opinion of my generosity and justice, as to trust their persons in my hands: that whatever they took from me should be returned when I left the country, or paid for at the rate which I would set upon them. I took up the two officers in my hands, put them first into my coat-pockets, and then into every other pocket about me, except my two fobs, and another secret pocket which I had no mind should be searched, wherein I had some little necessaries of no consequence to any but myself. In one of my fobs there were a silver watch, and in the other a small quantity of gold in a purse. These gentlemen, having pen, ink, and paper about them, made an exact inventory of every thing they saw, and when they had done, desired I would set them down, that they might deliver it to the Emperor. This inventory I afterwards translated into English, and is word for word as follows.

Imprimis, in the right coat-pocket of the Great Man-Mountain (for so I interpret the words Quinbus Flestrin) after the strictest search, we found only one great piece of coarse cloth, large enough to be a foot-cloth for your majesty's chief room of state. In the left pocket, we saw a huge silver chest, with a cover of the same metal, which we, the searchers, were not able to lift. We desired it should be opened; and one of us stepping into it, found himself up to the mid leg in a sort of dust, some part whereof flying up to our faces, set us both a sneezing for several times together. In his right waistcoat-pocket, we found a prodigious bundle of thin white substances, folded one above another, about the bigness of three men, tied with a strong cable, and marked with black figures; which we humbly conceive to be writings, every letter almost half as large as the palm of our hands. In the left there was a sort of engine, from the back of which were extended twenty long poles, resembling the pallisado's before your majesty's court; wherewith we conjecture the Man-Mountain combs his head; for we did not always trouble him with questions, because we found it a great difficulty to make him understand us. In the large

COMMENTARY

Two officers search through Gulliver's pockets, although he keeps the contents of one pocket secret as it contains some personal belongings. The officers write down everything they see but, as they are unfamiliar with all the objects, they have to describe them rather than simply name them. We also learn that the Lilliputians have named Gulliver the Great Man-Mountain.

fobs: small pockets in a vest
no consequence: little importance
inventory: list
Imprimis: in the first place
pallisado's: fences made from stakes of wood

pocket on the right side of his middle cover (so I translate the word ranfu-lo, by which they meant my breeches), we saw a hollow pillar of iron, about the length of a man, fastened to a strong piece of timber, larger than the pillar; and upon one side of the pillar were huge pieces of iron sticking out, cut into strange figures; which we know not what to make of. In the left pocket, another engine of the same kind. In the smaller pocket on the right side, were several round flat pieces of white and red metal, of different bulk: some of the white, which seemed to be silver, were so large and heavy, that my comrade and I could hardly lift them. In the left pocket were two black pillars irregularly shaped: we could not, without difficulty, reach the top of them as we stood at the bottom of his pocket: one of them was covered, and seemed all of a piece; but at the upper end of the other, there appeared a white round substance, about twice the bigness of our heads. Within end of these was inclosed a prodigious plate of steel; which, by our orders, we obliged him to show us, because we apprehended they might be dangerous engines. He took them out of their cases, and told us, that in his own country his practice was to shave his beard with one of these, and to cut his meat with the other. There were two pockets which we could not enter: these he called his fobs; they were two large slits cut into the top of his middle cover, but squeezed close by the pressure of his belly. Out of the right fob hung a great silver chain, with a wonderful kind of engine at the bottom. We directed him to draw out whatever was at the end of the chain; which appeared to be a globe, half silver, and half of some transparent metal: for on the transparent side we saw certain strange figures circularly drawn, and thought we could touch them, until we found our fingers stopped with that lucid substance. He put this engine to our ears, which made an incessant noise like that of a water-mill. And we conjecture it is either some unknown animal, or the god that he worships: but we are more inclined to the latter opinion, because he assured us (if we understood him right, for he expressed himself very imperfectly) that he seldom did any thing without consulting it. He called it his oracle, and said it pointed out the time for every action of his life. From the left fob he took out

breeches: knee-length trousers
lucid: transparent
incessant: continuous
oracle: guide for future action

COMMENTARY
The officers continue to describe the contents of Gulliver's pockets.

a net almost large enough for a fisherman, but contrived to open and shut like a purse, and served him for the same use: we found therein several massy pieces of yellow metal, which if they be real gold, must be of immense value.

Having thus, in obedience to your majesty's commands, diligently searched all his pockets, we observed a girdle about his waist made of the hide of some prodigious animal; from which, on the left side, hung a sword of the length of five men; and on the right, a bag or pouch divided into two cells; each cell capable of holding three of your majesty's subjects. In one of these cells were several globes or balls of a most ponderous metal, about the bigness of our heads, and required a strong hand to lift them: the other cell contained a heap of certain black grains, but of no great bulk or weight, for we could hold above fifty of them in the palm of our hands.

This is an exact inventory of what we found about the body of the Man-Mountain; who used us with great civility, and due respect to your majesty's commission. Signed and sealed on the fourth day of the eighty-ninth moon of your majesty's auspicious reign.

Clefven Frelock, Marsi Frelock

When this inventory was read over to the Emperor, he directed me to deliver up the several particulars. He first called for my scimitar, which I took out, scabbard and all. In the meantime he ordered three thousand of his choicest troops, who then attended him, to surround me at a distance, with their bows and arrows just ready to discharge: but I did not observe it; for mine eyes were wholly fixed upon his majesty. He then desired me to draw my scimitar, which, although it had got some rust by the seawater, was in most parts exceedingly bright. I did so, and immediately all the troops gave a shout between terror and surprise; for the sun shone clear, and the reflexion dazzled their eyes, as I waved the scimitar to and fro in my hand. His majesty, who is a most magnanimous prince, was less daunted than I could expect; he ordered me to return it into the scabbard, and cast it on the ground as gently as I

COMMENTARY
The officers finish their description of Gulliver's belongings. The emperor asks first to see Gulliver's sword, which Gulliver draws to the astonishment of the crowd.

contrived: designed
massy: massive
diligently: carefully
cells: sections
ponderous: heavy
auspicious: fortunate
scimitar: curved sword
magnanimous: generous and noble
daunted: frightened

could, about six foot from the end of my chain. The next thing he demanded
was one of the hollow iron pillars, by which he meant my pocket-pistols. I
drew it out, and at his desire, as well as I could, expressed to him the use of it,
and charging it only with powder, which by the closeness of my pouch,
happened to escape wetting in the sea (an inconvenience that all prudent
mariners take special care to provide against), I first cautioned the Emperor
not to be afraid; and then I let it off in the air. The astonishment here was
much greater than at the sight of my scimitar. Hundreds fell down as if they
had been struck dead; and even the Emperor, although he stood his ground,
could not recover himself in some time. I delivered up both my pistols in the
same manner as I had done my scimitar, and then my pouch of powder and
bullets; begging him that the former might be kept from the fire; for it would
kindle with the smallest spark, and blow up his imperial palace into the air. I
likewise delivered up my watch, which the Emperor was very curious to see;
and commanded two of his tallest yeomen of the guards to bear it on a pole
upon their shoulders, as draymen in England do a barrel of ale. He was
amazed at the continual noise it made, and the motion of the minute-hand,
which he could easily discern; for their sight is much more acute than ours: he
asked the opinions of his learned men about him, which were various and
remote, as the reader may well imagine without my repeating; although indeed
I could not very perfectly understand them. I then gave up my silver and
copper money, my purse with nine large pieces of gold, and some smaller ones;
my knife and razor, my comb and silver snuff-box, my handkerchief and
journal book. My scimitar, pistols, and pouch, were conveyed in carriages to
his majesty's stores; but the rest of my goods were returned to me.

I had, as I before observed, one private pocket which escaped their search,
wherein there was a pair of spectacles (which I sometimes use for the weakness
of mine eyes) a pocket perspective, and several other little conveniences;
which being of no consequence to the Emperor, I did not think myself bound
in honour to discover; and I apprehended they might be lost or spoiled if I
ventured them out of my possession.

COMMENTARY
Gulliver shows the emperor his pistol
and fires it to the horror of the crowd.
He reveals the remainder of the
contents of his pockets, and the
emperor decides to take Gulliver's
weapons.

charging: filling
kindle: light
draymen: men who carry heavy objects
remote: abstract
pocket perspective: telescope

3

The author diverts the Emperor and his nobility of both sexes, in a very uncommon manner. The diversions of the court of Lilliput described. The author hath his liberty granted him upon certain conditions.

My gentleness and good behaviour had gained so far on the Emperor and his court, and indeed upon the army and people in general, that I began to conceive hopes of getting my liberty in a short time. I took all possible methods to cultivate this favourable disposition. The natives came by degrees to be less apprehensive of any danger from me. I would sometimes lie down, and let five or six of them dance on my hand. And at last the boys and girls would venture to come and play hide and seek in my hair. I had now made a good progress in understanding and speaking their language. The Emperor had a mind one day to entertain me with several of the country shows; wherein they exceed all nations I have known, both for dexterity and magnificence. I was diverted with none so much as that of the rope-dancers, performed upon a slender white thread, extended about two foot, and twelve inches from the ground. Upon which I shall desire liberty, with the reader's patience, to enlarge a little.

COMMENTARY

The Lilliputians are beginning to trust Gulliver, as he is working hard to please them in the hope that he will be released. He has now learned the language and often spends time observing the customs of the country.

diverts: entertains
uncommon: unusual
diversions: entertainments
conceive: have
cultivate: encourage
apprehensive of: worried about
dexterity: skill

FAST FORWARD: to page 34   ▶▶

This diversion is only practised by those persons who are candidates for great employments, and high favour, at court. They are trained in this art from their youth, and are not always of noble birth, or liberal education. When a great office is vacant, either by death or disgrace (which often happens) five or six of those candidates petition the Emperor to entertain his majesty and the court with a dance on the rope; and whoever jumps the highest without falling, succeeds in the office. Very often the chief ministers themselves are commanded to show their skill, and to convince the Emperor that they have not lost their faculty. Flimnap, the treasurer, is allowed to cut a caper on the strait rope, at least an inch higher than any other lord in the whole Empire.

employments: jobs
petition: ask
faculty: ability
cut a caper: do a dance
strait: tight

COMMENTARY
Gulliver learns that people looking for promotion at court in Lilliput have to show their skill in tightrope walking. The reader is left to decide what this tells us about the court.

I have seen him do the summerset several times together, upon a trencher fixed on the rope, which is no thicker than a common packthread in England. My friend Reldresal, principal secretary for private affairs, is, in my opinion, if I am not partial, the second after the treasurer; the rest of the great officers are much upon a par.

These diversions are often attended with fatal accidents, whereof great numbers are on record. I myself have seen two or three candidates break a limb. But the danger is much greater, when the ministers themselves are commanded to show their dexterity; for, by contending to excel themselves and their fellows, they strain so far, that there is hardly one of them who hath not received a fall, and some of them two or three. I was assured, that a year or two before my arrival, Flimnap would have infallibly broke his neck, if one of the *king's cushions*, that accidentally lay on the ground, had not weakened the force of his fall.

There is likewise another diversion, which is only shown before the Emperor and Empress, and first minister, upon particular occasions. The Emperor lays on a table three fine silken threads of six inches long. One is blue, the other red, and the third green. These threads are proposed as prizes, for those persons whom the Emperor hath a mind to distinguish by a peculiar mark of his favour. The ceremony is performed in his majesty's great chamber of state; where the candidates are to undergo a trial of dexterity very different from the former; and such as I have not observed the least resemblance of in any other country of the old or the new world. The Emperor holds a stick in his hands, both ends parallel to the horizon, while the candidates advancing one by one, sometimes leap over the stick, sometimes creep under it backwards and forwards several times, according as the stick is advanced or depressed. Sometimes the Emperor holds one end of the stick, and his first minister the other; sometimes the minister has it entirely to himself. Whoever performs his part with most agility, and holds out the longest in leaping and creeping, is rewarded with the blue-coloured silk; the red is given to the next, and the green to the third, which they all wear girt twice round about the

COMMENTARY

Gulliver explains that people often hurt themselves in attempting to win the emperor's favor. Lilliputians can also win the honor of a colored thread from the emperor by being the best at jumping over or walking under a stick held by the emperor. As readers, we might want to think about what this tells us about the relationship between the emperor and his people.

summerset: somersault
trencher: wooden board
partial: biased
much upon a par: fairly equal
dexterity: skill
infallibly: certainly
distinguish: reward
advanced or depressed: raised or lowered

▶▶ middle; and you see few great persons about this court, who are not adorned with one of these girdles.

The horses of the army, and those of the royal stables, having been daily led before me, were no longer shy, but would come up to my very feet, without starting. The riders would leap them over my hand as I held it on the ground; and one of the Emperor's huntsmen, upon a large courser, took my foot, shoe and all; which was indeed a prodigious leap. I had the good fortune to divert the Emperor one day, after a very extraordinary manner. I desired he would order several sticks of two foot high, and the thickness of an ordinary cane, to be brought me; whereupon his majesty commanded the master of his woods to give directions accordingly; and the next morning six woodsmen arrived with as many carriages, drawn by eight horses each. I took nine of these sticks, and fixing them firmly in the ground in a quadrangular figure, two foot and a half square; I took four other sticks and tied them parallel at each corner, about two foot from the ground; then I fastened my handerkerchief to the nine sticks that stood erect; and extended it on all sides, till it was as tight as the top of a drum; and the four parallel sticks rising about five inches higher than the handkerchief, served as ledges on each side. When I had finished my work, I desired the Emperor to let a troop of his best horse, twenty-four in number, come and exercise upon this plain. His majesty approved of the proposal and I took them up one by one in my hands, ready mounted and armed, with the proper officers to exercise them. As soon as they got into order, they divided into two parties, performed mock skirmishes, discharged blunt arrows, drew

---

REWIND: . . . one of these girdles.
Gulliver describes two ways in which Lilliputians can gain the emperor's approval. The first is to show one's skill in performing acrobatics on a tightrope: Those who do well in this are given important jobs at court. The second ways is to leap over or crawl under a stick held out by the emperor: Those who are most skillful at this win colored silken threads to wear as trophies.

---

girdles: sashes
courser: swift horse
quadrangular: four-sided
skirmishes: minor battles

COMMENTARY
Using some sticks and his handkerchief, Gulliver builds a platform on which the Lilliputians can hold mock fights on horseback.

their swords, fled and pursued, attacked and retired; and in short discovered the best military discipline I ever beheld. The parallel sticks secured them and their horses from falling over the stage; and the Emperor was so much delighted that he ordered this entertainment to be repeated several days; and once was pleased to be lifted up, and give the word of command; and, with great difficulty, persuaded even the Empress herself to let me hold her in her close chair, within two yards of the stage, from whence she was able to take a full view of the whole performance. It was my good fortune that no ill accident happened in these entertainments; only once a fierce horse that belonged to one of the captains, pawing with his hoof struck a hole in my handkerchief and his foot slipping, he overthrew his rider and himself; but I immediately relieved them both: for covering the hole with one hand, I set down the troop with the other, in the same manner as I took them up. The horse that fell was strained in the left shoulder, but rider got no hurt; and I repaired my handkerchief as well as I could: however, I would not trust to the strength of it any more in such dangerous enterprizes.

COMMENTARY

The emperor is so impressed by the platform that he orders that the fights be repeated several times. However, they come to an end due to an accident in which a horse puts a hoof through the handkerchief.

close chair: chair carried on two poles

About two or three days before I was set at liberty, as I was entertaining the court with these kinds of feats, there arrived an express to inform his majesty, that some of his subjects riding near the place where I was first taken up, had seen a great black substance lying on the ground, very oddly shaped, extending its edges round as wide as his majesty's bedchamber, and rising up in the middle as high as a man: that it was no living creature, as they at first apprehended; for it lay on the grass without motion; and some of them had walked round it several times: that by mounting upon each others shoulders, they had got to the top, which was flat and even; and, stamping upon it, they found it was hollow within: that they humbly conceived it might be something belonging to the Man-Mountain; and if his majesty pleased, they would undertake to bring it with only five horses. I presently knew what they meant; and was glad at heart to receive this intelligence. It seems, upon my first reaching the shore, after our shipwreck, I was in such confusion, that before I came to the place where I went to sleep, my hat, which I had fastened with a string to my head while I was rowing, and had stuck on all the time I was swimming, fell off after I came to land; the string, as I conjecture, breaking by some accident which I never observed, but thought my hat had been lost at sea. I entreated his imperial majesty to give orders it might be brought to me as soon as possible, describing to him the use and the nature of it: and the next day the waggoners arrived with it, but not in a very good condition; they bored two holes in the brim, within an inch and half of the edge, and fastened two hooks in the holes; these hooks were tied by a long cord to the harness, and thus my hat was dragged along for half an English mile: but the ground in that country being extremely smooth and level, it received less damage than I expected.

Two days after this adventure, the Emperor having ordered that part of his army, which quarters in and about his metropolis, to be in a readiness, took a fancy of diverting himself in a very singular manner. He desired I would stand like a colossus, with my legs as far asunder as I conveniently could. He then commanded his general (who was an old experienced leader, and a great patron

---

apprehended: understood
entreated: asked
singular: original
colossus: a huge Greek statue
asunder: apart

COMMENTARY
A strange object is discovered near where Gulliver was first discovered by the Lilliputians. Gulliver eventually works out that it is his hat and it is returned to him.

of mine) to draw up the troops in close order, and march them under me; the foot by twenty-four in a breast, and the horse by sixteen, with drums beating, colours flying, and pikes advanced. This body consisted of three thousand foot, and a thousand horse. His majesty gave orders, upon pain of death, that every soldier in his march should observe the strictest decency with regard to

my person; which, however, could not prevent some of the younger officers from turning up their eyes as they passed under me. And, to confess the truth, my breeches were at that time in so ill a condition, that they afforded some opportunities for laughter and admiration.

I had sent so many memorials and petitions for my liberty, that his majesty at length mentioned the matter first in the cabinet, and then in a full council; where it was opposed by none, except Skyresh Bolgolam, who was pleased, without any provocation, to be my mortal enemy. But it was carried against him by the whole board, and confirmed by the Emperor. That minister was Galbet, or admiral of the realm; very much in his master's confidence, and a person well versed in affairs, but of a morose and sour complection. However,

COMMENTARY

Gulliver acts as a giant archway by standing with legs apart as a military procession passes underneath him. He finds this very embarrassing. Following this, his desire for freedom is once again debated by the government and it is decided that he will be unchained. Only one person objects: his enemy in court, Skyresh Bolgolam.

memorials: written requests
provocation: cause
mortal enemy: deadly enemy
morose: bad-tempered

he was at length persuaded to comply; but prevailed that the articles and conditions upon which I should be set free, and to which I must swear, should be drawn up by himself. These articles were brought to me by Skyresh Bolgolam in person, attended by two under secretaries, and several persons of distinction. After they were read, I was demanded to swear to the performance of them; first in the manner of my own country, and afterwards in the method prescribed by their laws; which was to hold my right foot in my left hand, to place the middle finger of my right hand on the crown of my head, and my thumb on the tip of my right ear. But, because the reader may perhaps be curious to have some idea of the style and manner of expression peculiar to that people, as well as to know the articles upon which I recovered my liberty; I have made a translation of the whole instrument, word for word, as near as I was able; which I here offer to the public.

Golbasto Momaren Evlame Gurdilo Shefin Mully Ully Gue, most mighty Emperor of Lilliput, delight and terror of the universe, whose dominions extend five thousand blustrugs, (about twelve miles in circumference) to the extremities of the globe: monarch of all monarchs: taller than the sons of men; whose feet press down to the centre, and whose head strikes against the sun: at whose nod the princes of the earth shake their knees; pleasant as the spring, comfortable as the summer, fruitful as autumn, dreadful as winter. His most sublime majesty proposeth to the Man-Mountain, lately arrived at our celestial dominions, the following articles, which by a solemn oath he shall be obliged to perform.

First, the Man-Mountain shall not depart from our dominions, without our licence under our great seal.

Secondly, he shall not presume to come into our metropolis, without our express order; at which time, the inhabitants shall have two hours warning, to keep within their doors.

Thirdly, the said Man-Mountain shall confine his walks to our principal high roads; and not offer to walk or lie down in a meadow, or field of corn.

comply: agree
prevailed: succeeded in persuading them
to the performance of them: to carry them out
instrument: document
dominions: lands
sublime: noble
celestial: heavenly

COMMENTARY
Skyresh Bolgolam finally agrees to Gulliver's release on certain conditions. These include the following: Gulliver must get a license if he ever wants to leave the country; he must gain permission to go into the city; and he must stick to main roads and not walk across fields or meadows.

Fourthly, as he walks the said roads, he shall take the utmost care not to trample upon the bodies of any of our loving subjects, their horses, or carriages; nor take any of our said subjects into his hands, without their own consent.

Fifthly, if an express require extraordinary dispatch; the Man-Mountain shall be obliged to carry in his pocket the messenger and horse, a six days journey once in every moon, and return the said messenger back (if so required) safe to our imperial presence.

Sixthly, he shall be our ally against our enemies in the island of Blefuscu, and do his utmost to destroy their fleet, which is now preparing to invade us.

Seventhly, that the said Man-Mountain shall, at his times of leasure, be aiding and assisting our workmen, in helping to raise certain great stones, towards covering the wall of the principal park, and our other royal buildings.

Eighthly, that said Man-Mountain shall, in two moons' time, deliver in an exact survey of the circumference of our dominions, by a computation of his own paces round the coast.

Lastly, that upon his solemn oath to observe all the above articles, the said Man-Mountain shall have a daily allowance of meat and drink, sufficient for the support of 1728 of our subjects; with free access to our royal person, and other marks of our favour. Given at our palace at Belfaborac the twelfth day of the ninety-first moon of our reign.

I swore and subscribed to these articles with great cheerfulness and content, although some of them were not so honourable as I could have wished; which proceeded wholly from the malice of Skyresh Bolgolam the high admiral: whereupon my chains were immediately unlocked, and I was at full liberty: the Emperor himself, in person, did me the honour to be by me at the whole ceremony. I made my acknowledgements, by prostrating myself at his majesty's feet: but he commanded me to rise; and after many gracious expressions, which, to avoid the censure of vanity, I shall not repeat; he added, that he hoped I should prove a useful servant, and well deserve all the favours he had already conferred upon me, or might do for the future.

COMMENTARY

The other conditions for Gulliver's release are as follows: He must take great care as he moves around the kingdom so as not to tread on anyone; he must be available for carrying messengers long distances; he must defend Lilliput from its enemies; and he must carry out certain tasks, such as measuring the kingdom and assisting in building work. As a reward for this work, he will be given a daily allowance of food. Gulliver accepts all the conditions, although he thinks some of them are a little unfair. However, as soon as he is unchained he thanks the emperor.

dispatch: speed
censure: criticism
conferred upon: granted

The reader may please to observe, that in the last article for the recovery of my liberty, the Emperor stipulates to allow me a quantity of meat and drink, sufficient for the support of 1728 Lilliputians. Some time after, asking a friend at court how they came to fix on that determinate number, he told me, that his majesty's mathematicians, having taken the height of my body by the help of a quadrant, and finding it to exceed theirs in the proportion of twelve to one, they concluded from the similarity of their bodies, that mine must contain at least 1728 of theirs, and consequently would require as much food as was necessary to support that number of Lilliputians. By which, the reader may conceive an idea of the ingenuity of that people, as well as the prudent and exact economy of so great a prince.

stipulates: guarantees
quadrant: an instrument for measuring
    angles
ingenuity: cleverness

COMMENTARY
Gulliver tells the reader how impressed he is with the Lilliputians' mathematical skills in working out exactly how much he should be fed.

4

Look out for . . .
- **the description of Mildendo, the capital of Lilliput.**
- **the arguments between the political parties and between Lilliput and Blefuscu, a nearby country. What do you think Swift thinks of these arguments?**

Mildendo, the metropolis of Lilliput, described, together with the Emperor's palace. A conversation between the author and a principal secretary, concerning the affairs of that Empire: the author's offers to serve the Emperor in his wars.

The first request I made after I had obtained my liberty, was, that I might have licence to see Mildendo, the metropolis; which the Emperor easily granted me, but with a special charge to do no hurt, either to the inhabitants, or their houses. The people had notice by proclamation of my design to visit the town. The wall which encompassed it, is two foot and a half high, and at least eleven inches broad, so that a coach and horses may be driven very safely round it; and it is flanked with strong towers at ten foot distance. I stept over the great Western gate, and passed very gently, and sideling through the two principal streets, only in my short waistcoat, for fear of damaging the roofs and eaves of the houses with the skirts of my coat. I walked with the utmost circumspection, to avoid treading on any stragglers, who might remain in the streets, although the orders were very strict, that all people should keep in

COMMENTARY
Gulliver gains permission to visit Mildendo, the capital. Gulliver explains that all the people of the city had to keep off the streets during his visit in case they were trodden on.

have licence: be allowed
encompassed: surrounded
it is flanked with: on its sides it has
sideling: sideways
eaves: roof edges
circumspection: care

their houses, at their own peril. The garret windows and tops of houses were so crowded with spectators, that I thought in all my travels I had not seen a more populous place. The city is an exact square, each side of the wall being five hundred foot long. The two great streets which run cross and divide it into four quarters, are five foot wide. The lanes and alleys which I could not enter, but only viewed them as I passed, are from twelve to eighteen inches. The town is capable of holding five hundred thousand souls. The houses are from three to five stories. The shops and markets well provided.

The Emperor's palace is in the centre of the city, where the two great streets meet. It is inclosed by a wall of two foot high, and twenty foot distant from the buildings. I had his majesty's permission to step over this wall; and the space being so wide between that and the palace, I could easily view it on every side. The outward court is a square of forty foot, and includes two other courts: in the inmost are the royal apartments, which I was very desirous to see, but found it extremely difficult; for the great gates, from one square into

garret: attic
more populous place: place with a larger
    population
cross: across
souls: people

COMMENTARY
Gulliver describes Mildendo and the outside of the emperor's palace.

another, were but eighteen inches high, and seven inches wide. Now the buildings of the outer court were at least five foot high, and it was impossible for me to stride over them, without infinite damage to the pile, although the walls were strongly built of hewn stone, and four inches thick. At the same time, the Emperor had a great desire that I should see the magnificence of his palace: but this I was not able to do till three days after, which I spent in cutting down with my knife some of the largest trees in the royal park, about an hundred yards distance from the city. Of these trees I made two stools, each about three foot high, and strong enough to bear my weight. The people having received notice a second time, I went again through the city to the palace, with my two stools in my hands. When I came to the side of the outer court, I stood upon one stool, and took the other in my hand: this I lifted over the roof, and gently set it down on the space between the first and second court, which was eight foot wide. I then stept over the buildings very conveniently from one stool to the other, and drew up the first after me with a hooked stick. By this contrivance I got into the inmost court; and lying down upon my side, I applied my face to the windows of the middle stories, which were left open on purpose, and discovered the most splendid apartments that can be imagined. There I saw the Empress, and the young princes in their several lodgings, with their chief attendants about them. Her imperial majesty was pleased to smile very graciously upon me, and gave me out of the window her hand to kiss.

But I shall not anticipate the reader with farther descriptions of this kind, because I reserve them for a greater work, which is now almost ready for the press; containing a general description of this Empire, from its first erection, though a long series of princes, with a particular account of their wars and politicks, laws, learning, and religion; their plants and animals, their peculiar manners and customs, with other matters very curious and useful; my chief design at present being only to relate such events and transactions as happened to the public, or to myself, during a residence of about nine months in that Empire.

COMMENTARY
To see inside the palace, Gulliver builds two wooden stools, which he uses to step over the five-foot buildings that surround the main apartments. The palace apartments appear splendid to Gulliver and it is as though he is looking into a doll's house.

pile: buildings
received notice: been warned
contrivance: method
anticipate: jump the gun with

FAST FORWARD: to page 46

One morning, about a fortnight after I had obtained my liberty, Reldresal, principal secretary (as they style him) of private affairs, came to my house, attended only by one servant. He ordered his coach to wait at a distance, and desired I would give him an hour's audience; which I readily consent to, on account of his quality, and personal merits, as well of the many good offices he had done me during my solicitations at court. I offered to lie down, that he might the more conveniently reach my ear; but he chose rather to let me hold him in my hand during our conversation. He began with compliments on my liberty; said, he might pretend to some merit in it; but, however, added, that if it had not been for the present situation of things at court, perhaps I might not have obtained it so soon. For, *said he*, as flourishing a condition as we appear to be to foreigners, we labour under two mighty evils; a violent faction at home, and the danger of an invasion by a most potent enemy from abroad. As to the first, you are to understand, that for above seventy moons past, there have been struggling parties in this Empire, under the names of *Tramecksan*, and *Slamecksan*, from the high and low heels on their shoes, by which they distinguish themselves.

It is alleged indeed, that the high heels are most agreeable to our ancient constitution: but however this be, his majesty hath determined to make use of only low heels in the administration of the government, and all offices in the gift of the crown; as you cannot but observe; and particularly, that his majesty's imperial heels are lower at least by a *drurr* than any of his court (*drurr* is a measure about the fourteenth part of an inch). The animosities between these two parties run so high, that they will neither eat nor drink, nor talk with each other. We compute the *Tramecksan*, or high heels, to exceed us in number; but the power is wholly on our side. We apprehend his imperial highness, the heir to the crown, to have some tendency towards the high heels; at least we can

COMMENTARY
About two weeks later, Reldresal, a government minister who is generally on Gulliver's side, visits him. He explains to Gulliver that Lilliput faces two threats. The first is the violent disagreements between the two main political parties who show their difference by wearing low- or high-heeled shoes. The present emperor seems to favor the low-heeled party, while it is suspected that his son, the heir to the throne, has sympathies with the high-heeled party.

audience: attention   *faction*: group
solicitations: requests   *constitution*: way of being governed
flourishing: good   *animosities*: disagreements

plainly discover one of his heels higher than the other; which gives him a hobble in his gait. Now, in the midst of these intestine disquiets, we are threatened with an invasion from the island of Blefuscu, which is the other great Empire of the universe, almost as large and powerful as this of his majesty. For as to what we have heard you affirm, that there are other kingdoms and states in the world, inhabited by human creatures as large as yourself, our philosophers are in much doubt; and would rather conjecture that you dropped from the moon, or one of the stars; because it is certain, that an hundred mortals of your bulk, would, in a short time, destroy all the fruits and cattle of his majesty's dominions. Besides, our histories of six thousand moons make no mention of any other regions, than the two great Empires of Lilliput and Blefuscu. Which two mighty powers have, as I was going to tell you, been engaged in a most obstinate war for six and thirty moons past. It began upon the following occasion. It is allowed on all hands, that the primitive way of breaking eggs before we eat them, was upon the larger end: but his present majesty's grandfather, while he was a boy, going to eat an egg, and breaking it according to the ancient practice, happened to cut one of his fingers. Whereupon the Emperor, his father, published an edict, commanding all his subjects, upon great penalties, to break the smaller end of their eggs. The people have so highly resented the law, that our histories tell us, there have been six rebellions raised on that account; wherein one Emperor lost his life, and another his crown. These civil commotions were constantly fomented by the monarchs of Blefuscu; and when they were quelled, the exiles always fled for refuge to that Empire. It is computed, that eleven thousand persons have, at several times, suffered death, rather than submit to break their eggs at the smaller end. Many hundred large volumes have been published upon this controversy; but the books of the Big-Endians have been long forbidden, and the whole party rendered incapable by law of holding employments. During the course of these troubles, the Emperors of Blefuscu did frequently expostulate by their ambassadors, accusing us of making a schism in religion, by offending against a fundamental doctrine of our great prophet Lustrog, the

COMMENTARY

The second threat facing Lilliput is of an invasion by the nearby empire of Blefuscu. Reldresal explains how the wars with Blefuscu started over a disagreement as to whether a boiled egg should be broken on the big end or the small end before it is eaten. This disagreement has caused civil wars in Lilliput, which have always been stirred up by the people from Blefuscu. As readers, we need to think about what Swift is saying to us about the kind of things that cause arguments between political parties and countries.

gait: walk
intestine: internal
civil commotions: civil wars
fomented: stirred up
quelled: controlled
controversy: disagreement
expostulate: argue
schism: split
fundamental doctrine: basic
   principle

fifty-fourth chapter of the *Brundrecal* (which is their Alcoran). This, however, is thought to be a mere strain upon the text: for the words are these; *that all true believers shall break their eggs at the convenient end*: and which is the convenient end, seems, in my humble opinion, to be left to every man's conscience, or at least in the power of the chief magistrate to determine. Now the Big-Endian exiles have found so much credit in the Emperor of Blefuscu's court; and so much private assistance and encouragement from their party here at home, that a bloody war hath been carried on between the two Empires for six and thirty moons with various success; during which time we have lost forty capital ships, and a much greater number of smaller vessels, together with thirty thousand of our best seamen and soldiers; and the damage received by the enemy is reckoned to be somewhat greater than ours. However, they have now equipped a numerous fleet, and are just preparing to make a descent upon us: and his imperial majesty, placing great confidence in your valour and strength, hath commanded me to lay this account of his affairs before you.

   I desired the secretary to present my humble duty to the Emperor, and to let me know, that I thought it would not become me, who was a foreigner, to interfere with parties; but I was ready, with the hazard of my life, to defend his ▶▶ person and state against all invaders.

REWIND: . . . against all invaders.
Gulliver receives a visit from Reldresal, the principal secretary of private affairs, who has been sent by the emperor. He explains to Gulliver that Lilliput is faced by two threats. The first is the conflict between the two main political parties, which is getting increasingly vicious. The second is the threat of an attack by the nearby empire of Blefuscu, which has built up a superior fleet of ships. Gulliver promises to help defend Lilliput.

◀◀

Alcoran: Koran, the sacred book of Islam
strain: twist
valour: bravery
hazard: risk

COMMENTARY
Reldresal finishes his explanation of the quarrel between Lilliput and Blefuscu and says that he has been sent by the emperor to ask for Gulliver's help in these conflicts. Gulliver agrees to defend Lilliput but states that he does not want to get involved in its political affairs.

5

The author by an extraordinary stratagem prevents an invasion. A high title of honour is conferred upon him. Ambassadors arrive from the Emperor of Blefuscu and sue for peace. The Empress's apartment on fire by an accident; the author instrumental in saving the rest of the palace.

The Empire of Blefuscu, is an island situated to the north-north-east side of Lilliput, from whence it is parted only by a channel of eight hundred yards wide. I had not yet seen it, and upon this notice of an intended invasion, I avoided appearing on that side of the coast, for fear of being discovered by some of the enemies ships, who had received no intelligence of me; all intercourse between the two Empires having been strictly forbidden during the war, upon pain of death; and an embargo laid by our Emperor upon all vessels whatsoever. I communicated to his majesty a project I had formed of seizing the enemies whole fleet; which, as our scouts assured us, lay at anchor in the harbour ready to sail with the first fair wind. I consulted the most experienced seamen, upon the depth of the channel, which they had often plumbed; who told me, that in the middle at high water it was seventy *glumgluffs* deep, which is about six foot of European measure; and the rest of it fifty *glumgluffs* at most.

COMMENTARY

Gulliver explains that Blefuscu is an island eight hundred yards from Lilliput. He has kept away from the coast facing Blefuscu as he is a secret weapon. He tells us that he has a plan to steal the entire fleet from Blefuscu.

stratagem: plan
sue for: request
instrumental: plays a part
intercourse: communication
embargo: ban on movement
plumbed: measured using a line with a
    lead weight at the end

I walked to the north-east coast over against Blefuscu; where, lying down behind a hillock, I took out my small pocket perspective glass, and viewed the enemy's fleet at anchor, consisting of about fifty men of war, and a great number of transports: I then came back to my house, and gave order (for which I had a warrant) for a great quantity of the strongest cable and bars of iron. The cable was about as thick as packthread, and the bars of the length and size of a knitting-needle. I trebled the cable to make it stronger; and for the same reason I twisted three of the iron bars together, bending the extremities into a hook. Having thus fixed fifty hooks to as many cables, I went back to the north-east coast, and putting off my coat, shoes, and stockings, walked into the sea in my leathern jerken, about half an hour before high water. I waded with what haste I could, and swam in the middle about thirty yards until I felt the ground; I arrived at the fleet in less than half an hour. The enemy was so frighted when they saw me, that they leaped out of their ships, and swam to shore; where they could not be fewer than thirty thousand souls. I then took my tackling, and fastening a hook to the hole at the prow of each, I tied all the cords together at the end. While I was thus employed, the enemy discharged several thousand arrows, many of which stuck in my hands and face; and besides the excessive smart, gave me much disturbance in my work. My greatest apprehension was for mine eyes, which I should have infallibly lost, if I had not suddenly thought of an expedient. I kept, among other little necessaries, a pair of spectacles in a private pocket, which, as I observed before, had escaped the Emperor's searchers. These I took out, and fastened as strongly as I could upon my nose; and thus armed went on boldly with my work in spite of the enemy's arrows; many of which struck against the glasses of my spectacles, but without any other effect, further than a little to discompose them. I had now fastened all the hooks, and taking the knot in my hand, began to pull; but not a ship would stir, for they were all too fast held by their anchors; so that the boldest part of my enterprise remained. I therefore let go the cord, and leaving the hooks fastened to the ships, I resolutely cut with my knife the cables that fastened the anchors; receiving

---

extremities: ends
tackling: ropes
prow: front
expedient: a plan to get around the
    problem
discompose: disorder
resolutely: determinedly

COMMENTARY
Gulliver has a large number of cables made and then swims over to Blefuscu. He ties a cable to each ship and cuts their anchor ropes. During all of this he is constantly bombarded with tiny arrows by the frightened Blefuscu people. Gulliver puts on his glasses to protect his eyes.

above two hundred shots in my face and hands: then I took up the knotted end of the cables to which my hooks were tied; and with great ease drew fifty of the enemy's largest men of war after me.

The Blefuscdians, who had not the least imagination of what I intended, were at first confounded with astonishment. They had seen me cut the cables, and thought my design was only to let the ships run adrift, or fall foul on each other; but when they perceived the whole fleet moving in order, and saw me pulling at the end, they set up such a scream of grief and dispair, that it is almost impossible to describe or conceive. When I had got out of danger, I stopped a while to pick out the arrows that stuck in my hands and face, and rubbed on some of the same ointment that was given me at my first arrival, as I have formerly mentioned. I then took off my spectacles, and waiting about an hour until the tide was a little fallen, I waded through the middle with my cargo, and arrived safe at the royal port of Lilliput.

The Emperor and his whole court stood on the shore, expecting the issue of this great adventure. They saw the ships move forward in a large half-moon,

COMMENTARY
Gulliver tows the ships back toward Lilliput, leaving the Blefuscudians in despair. He rubs the Lilliputian's ointment into the wounds caused by the arrows.

fall foul on: crash into
issue: results

but could not discern me, who was up to my breast in water. When I advanced to the middle of the channel, they were yet more in pain because I was under water to my neck. The Emperor concluded me to be drowned, and that the enemy's fleet was approaching in a hostile manner: but he was soon eased of his fears, for the channel growing shallower every step I made, I came in a short time within hearing; and holding up the end of the cable by which the fleet was fastened, I cried in a loud voice, *long live the most puissant Emperor of Lilliput!* This great prince received me at my landing with all possible encomiums, and created me a *Nardac* upon the spot, which is the highest title of honour among them.

His majesty desired I would take some other opportunity of bringing all the rest of his enemy's ships into his ports. And so unmeasurable is the ambition of princes, that he seemed to think of nothing less than reducing the whole Empire of Blefuscu into a province, and governing it by a viceroy; of destroying the Big-Endian exiles, and compelling that people to break the smaller end of the eggs, by which he would remain sole monarch of the whole world. But I endeavoured to divert him from this design, by many arguments drawn from the topics of policy as well as justice: and I plainly protested, that I would never be an instrument of bringing a free and brave people into slavery. And when the matter was debated in council, the wisest part of the ministry were of my opinion.

This open bold declaration of mine was so opposite to the schemes and politics of his imperial majesty, that he could never forgive me: he mentioned it in a very artful manner at council, where, I was told, that some of the wisest appeared, at least by their silence, to be of my opinion; but others, who were my secret enemies, could not forbear some expressions, which by a side-wind reflected on me. And from this time began an intrigue between his majesty, and a junta of ministers maliciously bent against me, which broke out in less than two months, and had like to have ended in my utter destruction. Of so little weight are the greatest services to princes, when put into the balance with a refusal to gratify their passions.

COMMENTARY

As Gulliver approaches Lilliput, the Lilliputians at first only see the ships and think they are being attacked. However, they eventually see Gulliver, and on his arrival he is rewarded with the title of "Nardac." The emperor wants to make the most of this victory by totally conquering Blefuscu and getting rid of all his enemies. Gulliver disagrees with this plan, saying that it is not right to turn a whole nation into slaves. As a result, Gulliver loses favor with the emperor and from that point the emperor, who seems very ungrateful, begins to plot against him.

discern: see
puissant: powerful
encomiums: praises
province: territory ruled by the emperor
viceroy: governor
endeavoured to divert him from this design: attempted to persuade him not to carry out this plan
artful: crafty
side-wind: a side effect
intrigue: plot
junta: small political group

FAST FORWARD: to page 52 ▶▶

About three weeks after this exploit, there arrived a solemn embassy from Blefuscu, with humble offers of a peace; which was soon concluded upon conditions very advantageous to our Emperor; wherewith I shall not trouble the reader. There were six ambassadors, with a train of about five hundred persons; and their entry was very magnificent, suitable to the grandeur of their master, and the importance of their business. When their treaty was finished, wherein I did them several good offices by the credit I now had, or at least appeared to have at court; their excellencies, who were privately told how much I had been their friend, made me a visit in form. They began with many compliments upon my valour and generosity; invited me to that kingdom in the Emperor their master's name; and desired me to show them some proofs of my prodigious strength, of which they had heard so many wonders; wherein I readily obliged them but shall not interrupt the reader with the particulars.

When I had for some time entertained their excellencies to their infinite satisfaction and surprise, I desired they would do me the honour to present my most humble respects to the Emperor their master, the renown of whose virtues had so justly filled the whole world with admiration, and whose royal person I resolved to attend before I returned to my own country. Accordingly, the next time I had the honour to see our Emperor, I desired his general licence to wait on the Blefuscudian monarch, which he was pleased to grant me, as I could plainly perceive, in a very cold manner; but could not guess the reason, till I had a whisper from a certain person, that Flimnap and Bolgolam had represented my intercourse with those ambassadors, as a mark of disaffection, from which I am sure my heart was wholly free. And this was the first time I began to conceive some imperfect idea of courts and ministers.

It is to be observed, that these ambassadors spoke to me by an interpreter; the languages of both Empires differing as much from each other as any two in

COMMENTARY

A group of important people from Blefuscu arrive to sign a peace treaty, which will greatly benefit the Lilliputians. Gulliver talks with them and decides to visit Blefuscu in the future. He asks permission from the emperor, who agrees but is not happy. Gulliver's wish to visit Blefuscu is seen by some government ministers as the act of a traitor.

embassy: group of officials
disaffection: treachery

Europe, and each nation priding itself upon the antiquity, beauty, and energy of their own tongues, with an avowed contempt for that of their neighbour: yet our Emperor standing upon the advantage he had got by the seizure of their fleet, obliged them to deliver their credentials, and make their speech in the Lilliputian tongue. And it must be confessed, that from the great intercourse of trade and commerce between both realms, from the continual reception of exiles, which is mutual among them, and from the custom in each Empire to send their young nobility and richer gentry to the other, in order to polish themselves, by seeing the world, and understanding men and manners, there are few persons of distinction, or merchants, or seamen, who dwell in the maritime parts, but what can hold conversation in both tongues; as I found some weeks after, when I went to pay my respects to the Emperor of Blefuscu, which in the midst of great misfortunes, through the malice of my enemies, ▶▶ proved a very happy adventure to me, as I shall relate in its proper place.

The reader may remember, that when I signed those articles upon which I recovered my liberty, there were some which I disliked upon account of their being too servile, neither could anything but an extreme necessity have forced me to submit. But being now a *Nardac*, of the highest rank in that Empire, such offices were looked upon as below my dignity; and the Emperor (to do him justice) never once mentioned them to me. However, it was not long before I had an opportunity of doing his majesty, at least, as I then thought, a most signal service. I was alarmed at midnight with the cries of many hundred people at my door; by which being suddenly awaked, I was in some kind of

---

REWIND: . . . its proper place.
Gulliver describes the visit of the ambassadors of Blefuscu who wanted peace. Gulliver meets with them and arranges to visit their empire. The emperor of Lilliput agrees to this but has begun to doubt Gulliver's loyalty. Gulliver is also surprised to see that although the two empires hate each other they can speak in each other's language.

◀◀ ◀

---

antiquity: age
is mutual among them: they both do
maritime parts: coastal areas
servile: slavish
signal: original

COMMENTARY
During their visit the people from Blefuscu are forced to speak in Lilliputian in order to humiliate them. Gulliver also learns that when not at war people from both countries freely mix and learn from one another. This makes the wars between them seem even more pointless. Now that Gulliver is a Nardac, the conditions of his freedom are forgotten.

terror. I heard the word burglum repeated incessantly; several of the Emperor's court making their way through the crowd, intreated me to come immediately to the palace, where her imperial majesty's apartment was on fire, by the carelessness of a maid of honour, who fell asleep while she was reading a romance. I got up in an instant; and orders being given to clear the way before me; and it being likewise a moonshine night, I made a shift to get to the palace without trampling on any of the people. I found they had already applied ladders to the walls of the apartment, and were well provided with buckets, but the water was at some distance. These buckets were about the size of a large thimble, and the poor people supplied me with them as fast as they could; but the flame was so violent, that they did little good. I might easily have stifled it with my coat, which I unfortunately left behind me for haste,

maid of honour: queen's attendant

COMMENTARY
Gulliver describes how one night the palace caught fire through an accident. The Lilliputians were having no success in putting it out with their tiny buckets of water.

and came away only in my leathern jerkin. The case seemed wholly desperate and deplorable; and this magnificent palace would have infallibly been burnt down to the ground, if, by a presence of mind, unusual to me, I had not suddenly thought of an expedient. I had the evening before drank plentifully of a most delicious wine, called *glimigrim*, (the Blefuscudians call it *flunec*, but ours is esteemed the better sort) which is very diuretic. By the luckiest chance in the world, I had not discharged myself of any part of it. The heat I had contracted by coming very near the flames, and by my labouring to quench them, made the wine begin to operate my urine; which I voided in such a quantity and applied so well to the proper places, that in three minutes the fire was wholly extinguished, and the rest of that noble pile, which had cost so many ages in erecting, preserved from destruction.

It was now daylight, and I returned to my house, without waiting to congratulate with the Emperor, because, although I had done a very eminent piece of service, yet I could not tell how his majesty might resent the manner by which I had performed it: for, by the fundamental laws of the realm, it is capital in any person, of what quality soever, to make water within the precincts of the palace. But I was a little comforted by a message from his majesty, that he would give orders to the grand justiciary for passing my pardon in form; which, however, I could not obtain. And I was privately assured, that the Empress conceiving the greatest abhorrence of which I had done, removed to the most distance side of the court, firmly resolved that those buildings should never be repaired for her use; and, in the presence of her chief confidents, could not forbear vowing revenge.

---

esteemed: believed
diuretic: drug encouraging urination
voided: released
congratulate with: rejoice with
eminent: outstanding
capital in: punishable by death
abhorrence: disgust

COMMENTARY

As a desperate measure, Gulliver urinates on the fire. This is very successful, but he is worried that he will be punished as he has broken a Lilliputian law by urinating in the palace grounds. The emperor promises he will be pardoned, but the empress is so disgusted she refused to live in any building Gulliver has urinated on. This is another event that causes plotting against Gulliver.

6

Of the inhabitants of Lilliput; their learning, laws, and customs. The manner of educating their children. The author's way of living in that country. His vindication of a great lady.

Although I intend to leave the description of this Empire to a particular treatise, yet in the meantime I am content to gratify the curious reader with some general ideas. As the common size of the natives is somewhat under six inches, so there is an exact proportion in all other animals, as well as plants and trees: for instance, the tallest horses and oxen are between four and five inches in height, the sheep an inch and a half, more or less; their geese about the bigness of a sparrow; and so the several gradations downwards, till you come to the smallest, which, to my sight, were almost invisible; but nature hath adapted the eyes of the Lilliputian to all objects proper for their view: they see with great exactness, but at no great distance. And to show the sharpness of their sight towards objects that are near, I have been much pleased with observing a cook pulling a lark, which was not so large as a

COMMENTARY
Gulliver explains that not only are the people twelve times smaller than ordinary humans, but everything in the kingdom is roughly twelve times smaller.

vindication: defense
treatise: book on a particular subject
gradations: degrees
proper for their view: they need to see
pulling: taking the insides out of

common fly; and a young girl threading an invisible needle with invisible silk. Their tallest trees are about seven foot high; I mean some of those in the great royal park, the tops whereof I could but just reach with my fist clinched. The other vegetables are in the same proportion: but this I leave to the reader's imagination.

FAST FORWARD: to page 59   ▶▶

I shall say but little at present of their learning, which for many ages hath flourished in all its branches among them: but their manner of writing is very peculiar; being neither from the left to the right, like the Europeans; nor from the right to the left, like the Arabians; nor from up to down like the Chinese, nor from down to up, like the Cascagians; but aslant from one corner of the paper to the other, like ladies in England.

They bury their dead with their heads directly downwards; because they hold an opinion, that in eleven thousand moons they are all to rise again; in which period, the earth (which they conceive to be flat) will turn upside down, and by this means they shall, at their resurrection, be found ready standing on their feet. The learned among them confess the absurdity of this doctrine; but the practice still continues, in compliance to the vulgar.

There are some laws and customs in this Empire very peculiar; and if they were not so directly contrary to those of my own dear country, I should be tempted to say a little in their justification. It is only to be wished, that they were as well executed. The first I shall mention, relateth to informers. All crimes against the state, are punished here with the utmost severity; but if the person accused make his innocence plainly to appear upon his trial, the accuser is immediately put to an ignominious death; and out of his goods or lands, the innocent person is quadruply recompensed for the loss of his time, for the danger he underwent, for the hardship of his imprisonment, and for all

COMMENTARY
Gulliver explains some of the customs of the land. First he tells us that Lilliputians write diagonally rather than horizontally. Then he explains that the Lilliputians believe the earth is flat and that in the future all people will live again. Therefore they bury their dead upside down so that when they come back to life they will be standing the right way up. Gulliver then goes on to describe two laws. The first is that if someone is falsely accused of a crime he or she is given money to make up for it, whereas the false accuser is put to death.

Cascagians: an invented race of people
in compliance to: to suit
vulgar: common people
contrary: opposite

ignominious: disgraceful
quadruply recompensed: rewarded
     four times as much

the charges he hath been at in making his defence. Or, if that found be
deficient, it is largely supplied by the crown. The Emperor doth also confer on
him some public mark of his favour, and proclamation is made of his
innocence through the whole city.

They look upon fraud as a greater crime than theft, and therefore seldom
fail to punish it with death: for they allege, that care and vigilance, with a very
common understanding, may preserve a man's goods from thieves; but
honesty hath no fence against superior cunning: and since it is necessary that
there should be a perpetual intercourse of buying and selling, and dealing
upon credit; where fraud is permitted or connived at, or hath no law to punish
it, the honest dealer is always undone, and the knave gets the advantage. I
remember when I was once interceding with the king for a criminal who had
wronged his master of a great sum of money, which he had received by order,
and ran away with; and happening to tell his majesty, by way of extenuation,
that it was only a breach of trust; the Emperor thought it monstrous in me to
offer, as a defence, the greatest aggravation of the crime: and truly, I had little
to say in return, farther than the common answer, that different nations had
different customs; for, I confess, I was heartily ashamed.

Although we usually call reward and punishment the two hinges upon
which all government turns; yet I could never observe this maxim to be put in
practice by any nation, except that of Lilliput. Whoever can there bring
sufficient proof that he hath strictly observed the laws of his country for
seventy-three moons, hath a claim to certain privileges, according to his
quality and condition of life, with a proportionable sum of money out of a
fund appropriated for that use: he likewise acquires the title of *Snilpall*, or
Legal, which is added to his name, but doth not descend to his posterity. And
these people thought it a prodigious defect of policy among us, when I told
them that our laws were enforced only by penalties, without any mention of
reward. It is upon this account that the image of justice, in their courts of
judicature, is formed with six eyes, two before, as many behind, and on each
side one, to signify circumspection; with a bag of gold open in her right hand,

COMMENTARY

The second law Gulliver describes is
about those who cheat people out of
money. They are dealt with more
severely than thieves as they are not
only guilty of stealing but have broken
trust with someone. Gulliver explains
that in Lilliput people are not only
punished for breaking laws but also
rewarded for keeping them.

fence: defense
perpetual intercourse: continual exchange
connived at: plotted
knave: cheat
extenuation: making it appear less serious
greatest aggravation: worst part
seventy-three moons: about five and a half
   years
quality and condition of life: place in society
appropriated: put aside
posterity: children
judicature: justice
circumspection: prudence, caution

and a sword sheathed to her left, to show she is more disposed to reward than to punish.

In choosing persons for all employments, they have more regard to good morals than to great abilities: for, since government is necessary to mankind, they believe that the common size of human understanding is fitted to some station or other, and that providence never intended to make the management of public affairs a mystery, to be comprehended only by a few persons of sublime genius, of which there seldom are three born in an age: but, they suppose truth, justice, temperance, and the like, to be in every man's power; the practice of which virtues, assisted by experience and a good intention, would qualify any man for the service of his country, except where a course of study is required. But they thought the want of moral virtues was so far from being supplied by superior endowments of the mind, that employments could never be put into such dangerous hands as those of persons so qualified; and at least, that the mistakes committed by ignorance in a virtuous disposition, would never be of such fatal consequence to the public weal, as the practices of a man, whose inclinations led him to be corrupt, and had great abilities to manage, to multiply, and defend his corruptions.

In like manner, the disbelief of a divine providence renders a man uncapable of holding any public station: for, since kings avow themselves to be the deputies of providence, the Lilliputians think nothing can be more absurd than for a prince to employ such men as disown the authority under which he acteth.

In relating these and the following laws, I would only be understood to mean the original institutions, and not the most scandalous corruptions into which the people are fallen by the degenerate nature of man. For as to that infamous practice of acquiring great employments by dancing on the ropes, or badges of favour and distinction by leaping over sticks, and creeping under them; the reader is to observe, that they were first introduced by the grandfather of the Emperor now reigning; and grew to the present height, by the gradual increase of party and faction.

common size of human understanding is:
    normal abilities of humans are
temperance: restraint
want: lack
endowments: gifts
virtuous disposition: good frame of mind
weal: welfare
divine providence: God's care of his
    creation
avow: swear
deputies: servants or representatives
degenerate: degraded
infamous: shocking

COMMENTARY
In Lilliput people are employed on the basis of their honesty and goodness rather than according to their abilities. Anybody taking an important job must believe in God because the emperor believes he is God's servant and therefore anyone serving him must also believe they are serving God. Gulliver states, however, that though many of their laws are good, too many of their principles are never put into practice.

Ingratitude is among them a capital crime, as we read it to have been in some other countries: for they reason thus; that whoever makes ill returns to his benefactor, must needs be a common enemy to the rest of mankind, from whom he hath received no obligation; and therefore such a man is not fit to live.

Their notions relating to the duties of parents and children differ extremely from ours. For, since the conjunction of male and female is founded upon the great law of nature, in order to propagate and continue the species; the Lilliputians will needs have it, that men and women are joined together like other animals, by the motives of concupiscence; and that their tenderness towards their young, proceedeth from the like natural principle: for which reason they will never allow, that a child is under any obligation to his father for begetting him, or to his mother for bringing him into the world; which, considering the miseries of human life, was neither a benefit in itself, nor intended so by his parents, whose thoughts in their love-encounters were otherwise employed. Upon these, and the like reasonings, their opinion is, that parents are the last of all others to be trusted with the education of their own children. And therefore they have in every town public nurseries, where all parents, except cottagers and labourers, are obliged to send their infants of both sexes to be reared and educated when they come to the age of twenty moons; at which time they are supposed to have some rudiments of docility. These schools are of several kinds, suited to different qualities, and to both sexes. They have certain professors well skilled in preparing children for such a

---

REWIND: . . . fit to live.
Gulliver first describes some of the customs of Lilliput, such as the way that they write and bury their dead. He then goes on to describe some of the laws in Lilliput that he approves of. He also likes the way that people are employed because of their good character rather than their abilities. He points out, however, that many of these principles are not carried out in practice.

COMMENTARY

The Lilliputians also despise ungratefulness, which is punishable by death. Gulliver then describes the Lilliputian customs relating to parents and children. Children in Lilliput are brought up in state nurseries rather than by their parents. The reason given for this is that when a child is conceived the parents are thinking of the pleasure of sexual intercourse rather than the welfare of the child. Boys and girls are brought up separately, and each child is taught differently depending on the class of its parents.

benefactor: someone who supports or helps
conjunction: joining
propagate: breed
concupiscence: desire
the like natural principle: the same natural cause
begetting: creating
cottagers: a rural laborer
some rudiments of docility: basic discipline
professors: teachers

condition of life as befits the rank of their parents, and their own capacities as well as inclinations. I shall first say something of the male nurseries, and then of the female.

The nurseries for males of noble or eminent birth, are provided with grave and learned professors, and their several deputies. The clothes and food of the children are plain and simple. They are bred up in the principles of honour, justice, courage, modesty, clemency, religion, and love of their country: they are always employed in some business, except in the times of eating and sleeping, which are very short, and two hours for diversions, consisting of bodily exercises. They are dressed by men until four years of age, and then are obliged to dress themselves, although their quality be ever so great; and the women attendants, who are aged proportionately to ours at fifty, perform only the most menial offices. They are never suffered to converse with servants, but go together in small or greater numbers to take their diversions, and always in the presence of a professor, or one of his deputies; whereby they avoid those early bad impressions of folly and vice to which our children are subject. Their parents are suffered to see them only twice a year; the visit is not to last above an hour; they are allowed to kiss the child at meeting and parting; but a professor, who always standeth by on those occasions, will not suffer them to whisper, or use any fondling expressions, or bring any presents of toys, sweet-meats, and the like.

The pension from each family for the education and entertainment of a child, upon failure of due payment, is levied by the Emperor's officers.

The nurseries for children of ordinary gentlemen, merchants, traders, and handicrafts, are managed proportionately after the same manner; only those designed for trades are put out apprentices at seven years old, whereas those of persons of quality continue in their exercises until fifteen, which answers to one and twenty with us: but the confinement is gradually lessened for the last three years.

In the female nurseries, the young girls of quality are educated much like the males, only they are dressed by orderly servants of their own sex, but

grave: serious
menial offices: basic domestic jobs
converse: talk
diversions: recreation
fondling: tender
pension: payment
levied: taxed
confinement is: tight rules are

COMMENTARY
Education in Lilliput is very much about having the right moral values. Children are always accompanied by a teacher to prevent them from getting into trouble.

always in the presence of a professor or deputy, until they come to dress themselves, which is at five years old. And if it be found that these nurses ever presume to entertain the girls with frightful or foolish stories, or the common follies practised by chamber-maids among us; they are publicly whipped thrice about the city, imprisoned for a year, and banished for life to the most desolate part of the country. Thus the young ladies there are as much ashamed of being cowards and fools, as the men; and despise all personal ornaments beyond decency and cleanliness; neither did I perceive any difference in their education, made by their difference of sex, only that the exercises of the females were not altogether so robust; and that some rules were given them relating to domestic life, and a smaller compass of learning was enjoined them: for, their maxim is, that among people of quality, a wife should be always a reasonable and agreeable companion, because she cannot always be young. When the girls are twelve years old, which among them is the marriageable age, their parents or guardians take them home, with great expressions of gratitude to the professors, and seldom without tears of the young lady and her companions.

In the nurseries of females of the meaner sort, the children are instructed in all kinds of works proper for their sex, and their several degrees: those intended for apprentices are dismissed at seven years old, the rest are kept to eleven.

The meaner families who have children at these nurseries, are obliged, besides their annual pension, which is as low as possible, to return to the steward of the nursery a small monthly share of their gettings, to be a portion for the child; and therefore all parents are limited in their expences by the law. For the Lilliputians think nothing can be more unjust, than that people, in subservience to their own appetites, should bring children into the world, and leave the burthen of supporting them on the public. As to persons of quality, they give security to appropriate a certain sum for each child, suitable to their condition; and these funds are always managed with good husbandry, and the most exact justice.

COMMENTARY
The education of the girls is fairly similar to that of the boys, as they are expected to avoid silly "girlish" behavior. However, their physical exercise is less energetic and they have additional training in how to run a household. The children's education is funded by the parents, as they were responsible for bringing the children into the world.

thrice: three times
robust: energetic
compass: scope
maxim: principle
meaner: poorer
degrees: positions in society
gettings: earnings
portion: allowance
subservience: slavery
burthen: burden
security: a guarantee
husbandry: management skills

The cottagers and labourers keep their children at home, their business being only to till and cultivate the earth; and therefore their education is of little consequence to the public; but the old and diseased among them are supported by hospitals: for begging is a trade unknown in this Empire.

And here it may perhaps divert the curious reader, to give some account of my domestic, and my manner of living in this country, during a residence of nine months and thirteen days. Having a head mechanically turned, and being likewise forced by necessity, I had made for myself a table and chair convenient enough, out of the largest trees in the royal park. Two hundred sempstresses were employed to make me shirts, and linnen for my bed and table, all of the strongest and coarsest kind they could get; which, however, they were forced to quilt together in several folds; for the thickest was some degrees finer than lawn. Their linen is usually three inches wide, and three foot make a piece. The sempstresses took my measure as I lay on the ground, one standing at my neck, and another at my mid-leg, with a strong cord extended, that each held by the end, while the third measured the length of the cord

domestic: household arrangements
a head mechanically turned: skill in building
    things
sempstresses: women who make clothes

COMMENTARY
The only children not educated are the poorest, the children of farmworkers. It is assumed that they do not need educating for their job. However, there is no begging in Lilliput as the old and ill are looked after in hospitals. Gulliver then describes his household arrangements, including how he made a table and chair for himself and the way in which he was clothed.

with a rule of an inch long. Then they measured my right thumb, and desired no more; for by a mathematical computation, that twice round the thumb is once round the wrist, and so on to the neck and the waist; and by the help of my old shirt, which I displayed on the ground before them for a pattern, they fitted me exactly. Three hundred taylors were employed in the same manner to make me clothes; but they had another contrivance for taking my measure. I kneeled down, and they raised a ladder from the ground to my neck; upon this ladder one of them mounted and let fall a plum-line from my collar to the floor, which just answered the length of my coat; but my waist and arms I measured myself. When my clothes were finished, which was done in my house (for the largest of theirs would not have been able to hold them), they looked like the patchwork made by the ladies in England, only that mine were all of a colour.

I had three hundred cooks to dress my victuals, in little convenient huts built around my house, where they and their families lived, and prepared me two dishes apiece. I took up twenty waiters in my hand, and placed them on the table; an hundred more attended below on the ground, some with dishes of meat, and some with barrels of wine, and other liquors, slung on their shoulders; all which the waiters above drew up as I wanted, in a very ingenious manner, by certain cords, as we draw the bucket up a well in Europe. A dish of their meat was a good mouthful, and a barrel of their liquor a reasonable draught. Their mutton yields to ours, but their beef is excellent. I have had a sirloin so large, that I have been forced to make three bits of it; but this is rare. My servants were astonished to see me eat it bones and all, as in our country we do the leg of a lark. Their geese and turkeys I usually eat at a mouthful, and I must confess they far exceed ours. Of their smaller fowl I could take up twenty or thirty at the end of my knife.

One day his imperial majesty being informed of my way of living, desired that himself, and his royal consort, with the young princes of the blood of both sexes, might have the happiness (as he was pleased to call it) of dining with me. They came accordingly, and I placed them upon chairs of state on my

COMMENTARY

Gulliver continues to describe how clothes were made for him and then goes on to an explanation of his eating arrangements. The emperor and family visit Gulliver.

plum-line: a device used for measuring depth
yields to: is inferior to
royal consort: the queen

table, just over against me, with their guards about them. Flimnap the lord high treasurer attended there likewise, with his white staff; and I observed he often looked on me with a sour countenance, which I would not seem to regard, but eat more than usual, in honour to my dear country, as well as to fill the court with admiration. I have some private reasons to believe, that this visit from his majesty gave Flimnap an opportunity of doing me ill offices to his master. That minister had always been my secret enemy, although he outwardly caressed me more than was usual to the moroseness of his nature. He represented to the Emperor the low condition of his treasury; that he was forced to take up money at great discount; that exchequer bills would not circulate under nine per cent below par; that I had cost his majesty above a million and a half of *sprugs* (their greatest gold coin, about the bigness of a spangle); and upon the whole, that it would be advisable in the Emperor to take the first fair occasion of dismissing me.

his white staff: a sign of his position
caressed: flattered
moroseness: gloominess
exchequer bills would not circulate under nine per cent below par: the government was borrowing beyond its means

COMMENTARY
Flimnap, the treasurer, is also present at the royal visit. Gulliver explains that Flimnap has complained about how expensive Gulliver is.

FAST FORWARD: to page 66

I am here obliged to vindicate the reputation of an excellent lady, who was an innocent sufferer on my account. The treasurer took a fancy to be jealous of his wife, from the malice of some evil tongues, who informed him that her grace had taken a violent affection for my person; and the court-scandal ran for some time that she once came privately to my lodging. This I solemnly declare to be a most infamous falsehood, without any grounds, farther than that her grace was pleased to treat me with all innocent marks of freedom and friendship. I own she came often to my house, but always publicly, nor ever without three more in the coach, who were usually her sister and young daughter, and some particular acquaintance; but this was common to many other ladies of the court. And I still appeal to my servants round, whether they at any time saw a coach at my door without knowing what persons were in it. On those occasions, when a servant had given me notice, my custom was to go immediately to the door; and after paying my respects, to take up the coach and two horses very carefully in my hands (for if there were six horses, the postillion always unharnessed four), and place them on a table, where I had fixed a moveable rim quite round, of five inches high, to prevent accidents. And I have often had four coaches and horses at once on my table full of company, while I sat in my chair leaning my face towards them; and when I was engaged with one set, the coachmen would gently drive the others round my table. I have passed many an afternoon very agreeably in these conversations. But I defy the treasurer, or his two informers (I will name them, and let them make the best of it), Clustril and Drunlo, to prove that any person ever came to me incognito, except the secretary Reldresal, who was sent by express command of his imperial majesty, as I have before related. I should not have dwelt so long upon this particular, if it had not been a point wherein the reputation of a great lady is so nearly concerned, to say nothing of my

COMMENTARY

Flimnap thinks his wife is too fond of Gulliver and this makes him even more anxious to get rid of Gulliver. Gulliver says that whenever she visited him it was in the presence of other people and there was no possibility of an affair. He is very eager to protect the reputation of Flimnap's wife.

vindicate: defend
violent affection: strong desire
particular acquaintance: close friend
postillion: person who guides the horses of a carriage
incognito: in secret

own; although I had the honour to be a *Nardac*, which the treasurer himself is not; for all the world knows he is only a *Clumglum*, a title inferior by one degree, as that of a marquess is to a duke in England; yet I allow he preceded me in right of his post. These false informations, which I afterwards came to the knowledge of, by an accident not proper to mention, made the treasurer show his lady for some time an ill countenance, and me a worse: for although he were at last undeceived and reconciled to her, yet I lost all credit with him, and found my interest decline very fast with the Emperor himself, who was indeed too much governed by that favourite.

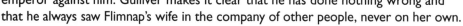

> **REWIND:** . . . by that favourite.
> Gulliver describes how Flimnap, the treasurer, became jealous of his wife's affection for Gulliver and how this made Flimnap turn the emperor against him. Gulliver makes it clear that he has done nothing wrong and that he always saw Flimnap's wife in the company of other people, never on her own.

undeceived: made aware of the truth
credit: favor
interest: favor

COMMENTARY
Because Flimnap is a favorite of the emperor, Gulliver's quarrel with him means that he is increasingly unpopular with the emperor.

7

The author being informed of a design to accuse him of high treason, makes his escape to Blefuscu. His reception there.

Before I proceed to give an account of my leaving this kingdom, it may be proper to inform the reader of a private intrigue which had been for two months forming against me.

I had been hitherto all my life a stranger to courts, for which I was unqualified by the meanness of my condition. I had indeed heard and read enough of the dispositions of great princes and ministers; but never expected to have found such terrible effects of them in so remote a country, governed, as I thought, by very different maxims from those in Europe.

When I was just preparing to pay my attendance on the Emperor of Blefuscu, a considerable person at court (to whom I had been very serviceable at a time when he lay under the highest displeasure of his imperial majesty) came to my house very privately at night in a close chair, and without sending

serviceable: helpful

COMMENTARY
Gulliver explains that he has learned from a friend at court about the plotting going on there. He is surprised because he thought better of the Lilliputians.

his name, desired admittance, the chairmen were dismissed; I put the chair, with his lordship in it, into my coat-pocket; and giving orders to a trusty servant to say I was indisposed and gone to sleep, I fastened the door of my house, placed the chair on the table, according to my usual custom, and sat down by it. After the common salutations were over, observing his lordship's countenance full of concern; and enquiring into the reason, he desired I would hear him with patience, in a matter that highly concerned my honour and my life. His speech was to the following effect, for I took notes of it as soon as he left me.

You are to know, said he, that several committees of council have been lately called in the most private manner on your account: and it is but two days since his majesty came to a full resolution.

You are very sensible that Skyris Bolgolam (*Galbet*, or high admiral) hath been your mortal enemy almost ever since your arrival. His original reasons I know not; but his hatred is much encreased since your great success against Blefuscu, by which his glory, as admiral, is obscured. This lord, in conjunction with Flimnap the high treasurer, whose enmity against you is notorious on account of his lady; Limtoc the general, Lalcon the chamberlain, and Balmuff the grand justiciary, have prepared articles of impeachment against you, for treason and other capital crimes.

This preface made me so impatient, being conscious of my own merits and innocence, that I was going to interrupt; when he entreated me to be silent; and thus proceeded.

Out of gratitude for the favours you have done me, I procured information of the whole proceedings, and a copy of the articles, wherein I venture my head for your service.

FAST FORWARD: to page 73

---

indisposed: unwell
salutations: greetings
resolution: decision
sensible: aware
obscured: hidden
enmity: hatred
chamberlain: the king's household
     manager
justiciary: judge
articles of impeachment: charges
procured: obtained
venture my head: risk my life

COMMENTARY
Gulliver's friend explains that certain members of the court have always despised him and that some are envious of his success against Blefuscu. They have therefore decided to accuse him of treason.

Articles of impeachment against Quinbus Flestrin (*the* Man-Mountain)

ARTICLE I

Whereas, by a statute made in the reign of his imperial majesty Calin Deffar Plune, it is enacted, that whoever shall make water within the precincts of the royal palace, shall be liable to the pains and penalties of high treason: notwithstanding, the said Quinbus Flestrin, in open breach of the said law, under colour of extinguishing the fire kindled in the apartment of his majesty's most dear imperial consort, did maliciously, traitorously, and devilishly, by discharge of his urine, put out the said fire kindled in the said apartment, lying and being within the precincts of the said royal palace; against the statute in that case provided, etc. against the duty, etc.

ARTICLE II

That the said Quinbus Flestrin having brought the imperial fleet of Blefuscu into the royal port, and being afterwards commanded by his imperial majesty to seize all the other ships of the said Empire of Blefuscu, and reduce that Empire to a province, to be governed by a viceroy from hence; and to destroy and put to death not only all the Big-Endian exiles, but likewise all the people of that Empire, who would not immediately forsake the Big-Endian heresy: he the said Flestrin, like a false traitor against his most auspicious, serene, imperial majesty, did petition to be excused from the said service, upon pretence of unwillingness to force the consciences, or destroy the liberties and lives of an innocent people.

ARTICLE III

That, whereas certain ambassadors arrived from the court of Blefuscu to sue for peace in his majesty's court: he the said Flestrin did, like a false traitor, aid, abet, comfort, and divert the said ambassadors, although he knew them to be servants to a prince who was lately an open enemy to his imperial majesty and in open war against his said majesty.

COMMENTARY

The four charges against Gulliver are
1. He urinated in the palace grounds.
2. He disagreed with the emperor over conquering Blefuscu.
3. He was kind to the Blefuscudian visitors.
4. He plans to visit Blefuscu.

statute: law
enacted: stated
within the precincts of the royal palace: within the palace walls
notwithstanding: even so
in open breach: in defiance
heresy: unofficial belief
auspicious: prosperous
serene: peaceful
abet: encourage

ARTICLE IV

That the said Quinbus Flestrin, contrary to the duty of a faithful subject, is now preparing to make a voyage to the court and Empire of Blefuscu, for which he hath received only verbal licence from his imperial majesty; and under colour of the said licence, doth falsely and traitorously intend to take the said voyage, and thereby to aid, comfort, and abet the Emperor of Blefuscu, so late an enemy, and in open war with his imperial majesty aforesaid.

There are some other articles, but these are the most important, of which I have read you an abstract.

In the several debates upon this impeachment, it must be confessed that his majesty gave many marks of his great lenity; often urging the services you had done him, and endeavouring to extenuate your crimes. The treasurer and admiral insisted that you should be put to the most painful and ignominious death, by setting fire on your house at night; and the general was to attend with twenty thousand men armed with poisoned arrows, to shoot you on the face and hands. Some of your servants were to have private orders to strew a poisonous juice on your shirts and sheets, which would soon make you tear your own flesh, and die in the utmost torture. The general came into the same opinion, so that for a long time there was a majority against you. But his majesty resolving, if possible, to spare your life, at last brought off the chamberlain.

Upon this incident, Reldresal, principal secretary for private affairs, who always approved himself your true friend, was commanded by the Emperor to deliver his opinion, which he accordingly did; and therein justified the good thoughts you have of him. He allowed your crimes to be great, but that still there was room for mercy, the most commendable virtue in a prince, and for which his majesty was so justly celebrated. He said, the friendship between you and him was so well known to the world, that perhaps the most honourable board might think him partial: however, in obedience to the

verbal licence: spoken agreement
an abstract: a summary
lenity: mercy
endeavouring to extenuate: attempting to
    excuse a little
ignominious: shameful
strew: spread
commendable: praiseworthy

COMMENTARY
Gulliver learns that the emperor was unwilling to put Gulliver to death and wanted to show that he was a merciful ruler. Gulliver's enemies, however, thought that he should be poisoned or burned to death. Gulliver's friend, Reldresal, felt that it would create a good impression if the emperor was seen to be merciful.

command he had received, he would freely offer his sentiments. That if his majesty, in consideration of your services, and pursuant to his own merciful disposition, would please to spare your life, and only give order to put out both your eyes; he humbly conceived, that by this expedient, justice might in some measure be satisfied, and all the world would applaud the lenity of the Emperor, as well as the fair and generous proceedings of those who have the honour to be his counsellors. That the loss of your eyes would be no impediment to your bodily strength, by which you might still be useful to his Majesty. That blindness is an addition to courage, by concealing dangers from us; that the fear you had for your eyes, was the greatest difficulty in bringing over the enemy's fleet, and it would be sufficient for you to see by the eyes of the ministers, since the greatest princes do no more.

This proposal was received with the utmost disapprobation by the whole board. Bolgolam, the admiral, could not preserve his temper; but rising up in fury, said, he wondered how the secretary durst presume to give his opinion for

COMMENTARY
Reldresal suggested to the emperor that Gulliver should be blinded rather than killed. This would show the emperor's mercy and would mean that Gulliver would still be strong enough to be useful to the emperor.

sentiments: feelings
pursuant to: following
impediment: obstacle
see by the eyes of: be guided by
disapprobation: disapproval

preserving the life of a traitor: that the services you had performed were, by all true reasons of state, the great aggravation of your crimes; that you, who were able to extinguish the fire, by discharge of urine in her majesty's apartment (which he mentioned with horror) might, at another time, raise an inundation by the same means, to drown the whole palace; and the same strength which enable you to bring over the enemy's fleet, might serve, upon the first discontent, to carry it back: that he had good reasons to think you were a Big-Endian in your heart; and as treason begins in the heart before it appears in overt acts; so he accused you as a traitor on that account, and therefore insisted you should be put to death.

The treasurer was of the same opinion; he showed to what streights his majesty's revenue was reduced by the charge of maintaining you, which would soon grow insupportable: that the secretary's expedient of putting out your eyes, was so far from being a remedy against this evil, that it would probably increase it, as it is manifest from the common practice of blinding some kind of fowl, after which they fed the faster, and grew sooner fat: that his sacred majesty, and the council, who are your judges, were in their own consciences fully convinced of your guilt; which was sufficient argument to condemn you to death, without the *formal proofs required by the strict letter of the law.*

But his imperial majesty fully determined against capital punishment, was graciously pleased to say, that since the council thought the loss of your eyes too easy a censure, some other may be inflicted hereafter. And your friend the secretary humbly desiring to be heard again, in answer to what the treasurer had objected concerning the great charge his majesty was at in maintaining you; said, that his excellency, who had the sole disposal of the Emperor's revenue, might easily provide against this evil, by gradually lessening your establishment; by which, for want of sufficient food, you would grow weak and faint, and lose your appetite, and consequently decay and consume in a few months; neither would the stench of your carcass be then so dangerous, when it should become more than half diminished; and immediately upon your death, five or six thousand of his majesty's subjects might, in two or three

---

great aggravation: worst part

inundation: flood

overt: open

to what streights his majesty's revenue was reduced: the poor state the emperor's finances had been reduced to

censure: punishment

disposal: charge

consume: waste away

COMMENTARY

Gulliver's enemies disagreed with Reldresal and again listed the charges against Gulliver and added that he was becoming too expensive to look after. They said that even though he had not actually gone over to the side of the Blefuscudians, it was enough that he had kind intentions toward them. Eventually the court had agreed to blind Gulliver and to starve him slowly to death.

days, cut your flesh from your bones, take it away by cart-loads, and bury it in distance parts to prevent infection; leaving the skeleton as a monument of admiration to posterity.

◀◀

Thus by the great friendship of the secretary, the whole affair was compromised. It was strictly enjoined, that the project of starving you by degrees should be kept a secret, but the sentence of putting out your eyes was entered on the books; none dissenting except Bolgolam the admiral, who being a creature of the Empress, was perpetually instigated by her majesty to insist upon your death, she having born perpetual malice against you, on account of that infamous and illegal method you took to extinguish the fire in her apartment.

In three days your friend the secretary will be directed to come to your house, and read before you the articles of impeachment; and then to signify the great lenity and favour of his majesty and council, whereby you are only condemned to the loss of your eyes, which his majesty doth not question you will gratefully and humbly submit to; and twenty of his majesty's surgeons will attend, in order to see the operation well performed, by discharging very sharp pointed arrows into the balls of your eyes, as you lie on the ground.

I leave to your prudence what measures you will take; and to avoid suspicion, I must immediately return in as private a manner as I came.

His lordship did so, and I remained alone, under many doubts and perplexities of mind.

REWIND: . . . admiration to posterity.

Gulliver's friend tells him of the plot against him. Gulliver has been accused of a number of things, including his urinating in the palace grounds and his friendliness toward Blefuscu. Gulliver's enemies want to kill him with fire or poison, while those more friendly to him suggest that he should only lose his eyes as a punishment. This punishment was finally agreed to, along with a decision to starve Gulliver slowly to death.

◀◀

COMMENTARY

Gulliver's friend says that the idea of starving him was to be kept a secret at court and that his eyes would be put out in three days' time. We also learn that the empress has been behind much of the plotting as she was still angry about Gulliver urinating on the palace fire.

to posterity: for the future
enjoined: commanded
creature: puppet
perpetually instigated: continually pressed
perplexities: confusions

It was a custom introduced by this prince and his ministry (very different, as I have been assured, from the practices of former times), that after the court had decreed any cruel execution, either to gratify the monarch's resentment, or the malice of a favourite; the Emperor always made a speech to his whole council, expressing his *great lenity and tenderness, as qualities known and confessed by all the world*. This speech was immediately published through the kingdom; nor did any thing terrify the people so much as those encomiums on his majesty's mercy; because it was observed, that the more these praises were enlarged and insisted on, the more *inhuman* was the punishment, and the *sufferer more innocent*. Yet, as to myself, I must confess, having never been designed for a courtier, either by my birth or education, I was so ill a judge of things, that I could not discover the lenity and favour of this sentence, but conceived it (perhaps erroneously) rather to be rigorous than gentle. I sometimes thought of standing my trial; for although I could not deny the facts alleged in the several articles, yet I hoped they would admit of some extenuations. But having in my life perused many state trials, which I ever observed to terminate as the judges thought fit to direct; I durst not rely on so dangerous a decision, in so critical a juncture, and against such powerful enemies. Once I was strongly bent upon resistance: for while I had liberty, the whole strength of that Empire could hardly subdue me, and I might easily with stones pelt the metropolis to pieces: but I soon rejected that project with horror, by remembering the oath I had made to the Emperor, that favours I received from him, and the high title of *Nardac* he conferred upon me. Neither had I so soon learned the gratitude of courtiers, to persuade myself that his majesty's present severities acquitted me of all past obligations.

At last I fixed upon a resolution, for which it is probable I may incur some censure, and not unjustly; for I confess I owe the preserving mine eyes, and consequently my liberty, to my own great rashness and want of experience: because if I had then known the nature of princes and ministers, which I have since observed in many other courts, and their methods of treating criminals less obnoxious than myself; I should with great alacrity and readiness have

---

encomiums: speeches of praise
erroneously: wrongly
rigorous: harsh
perused: watched
terminate: end
juncture: moment
bent: decided
present severities acquitted me of all past obligations: present harshness relieved me of the need to be grateful for past help
obnoxious: unpleasant

COMMENTARY

Gulliver tells us that he is always amazed that whenever the emperor passes harsh sentences on people, he always states how merciful he is being. He does, however, know that he would probably be unsuccessful at a trial as he feels that in law courts the sentence is often decided before the trial begins. Gulliver considers taking revenge on the Lilliputians but remembers the ways that they have helped him and feels that would be ungrateful. He confesses that his understanding of governments and the law is not great and asks that the reader forgive him.

submitted to so *easy* a punishment. But hurried on by the precipitancy of youth; and having his imperial majesty's licence to pay my attendance upon the Emperor of Blefuscu; I took this opportunity, before the three days were elapsed, to send a letter to my friend the secretary, signifying my resolution of setting out that morning for Blefuscu, pursuant to the leave I had got; and without waiting for an answer, I went to that side of the island where our fleet lay. I seized a large man of war, tied a cable to the prow, and lifting up the anchors, I stripped myself, put my clothes (together with my coverlet, which I carryed under my arm) into the vessel, and drawing it after me, between wading and swimming, arrived at the royal port of Blefuscu, where the people had long expected me: they lent me two guides to direct me to the capital city, which is of the same name; I held them in my hands until I came within two hundred yards of the gate; and desired them to signify my arrival to one of the secretaries, and let him know, I there waited his majesty's commands. I had an answer in about an hour, that his majesty, attended by the royal family, and great officers of the court, was coming out to receive me. I advanced a hundred

precipitancy: haste

COMMENTARY
Gulliver decides to escape to Blefuscu before the punishment can be carried out. He takes one of the biggest ships, puts his clothes in it, and swims across to Blefuscu, tugging the ship behind him.

yards. The Emperor, and his train, alighted from their horses, the Empress and ladies from their coaches, and I did not perceive they were in any fright or concern. I lay on the ground to kiss his majesty's and the Empress's hand. I told his majesty, that I was come according to my promise, and with the licence of the Emperor my master, to have the honour of seeing so mighty a monarch, and to offer him any service in my power, consistent with my duty to my own prince; not mentioning a word of my disgrace, because I had hitherto no regular information of it, and might suppose myself wholly ignorant of any such design; neither could I reasonably conceive that the Emperor would discover the secret while I was out of his power: wherein, however, it soon appeared I was deceived.

I shall not trouble the reader with the particular account of my reception at this court, which was suitable to the generosity of so great a prince; nor of the difficulties I was in for want of a house and bed, being forced to lie on the ground, wrapped up in my coverlet.

regular: official
design: plot
discover the secret: make known the plot

COMMENTARY
When Gulliver reaches Blefuscu he is greeted by the emperor and his people, and they seem very brave. He does not tell them of his problems in Lilliput.

Look out for . . .
- **the type of person the emperor of Blefuscu is. Is he like the emperor of Lilliput?**
- **Gulliver's changed attitude toward rulers.**

The author, by a lucky accident, finds means to leave Blefuscu; and, after some difficulties, returns safe to his native country.

Three days after my arrival, walking out of curiosity to the north-east coast of the island, I observed, about half a league off, in the sea, somewhat that looked like a boat overturned: I pulled off my shoes and stockings, and wading two or three hundred yards, I found the object to approach nearer by force of the tide; and then plainly saw it to be a real boat, which I supposed might, by some tempest, have been driven from a ship. Whereupon I returned immediately towards the city, and desired his imperial majesty to lend me twenty of the tallest vessels he had left after the loss of his fleet, and three thousand seamen under the command of his vice-admiral. This fleet sailed round, while I went back the shortest way to the coast where I first discovered the boat; I found the tide had driven it still nearer; the seamen were all provided with cordage, which I had beforehand twisted to a sufficient strength. When the ships came up, I stripped myself, and waded till I came within an

COMMENTARY
Gulliver sees a normal-size boat in the sea and he asks the people of Blefuscu to help him tow it in to land.

tempest: storm
cordage: cords

hundred yards of the boat; after which I was forced to swim till I got up to it.
The seamen threw me the end of the cord, which I fastened to a hole in the
forepart of the boat, and the other end to a man of war: but I found all my
labour to little purpose; for being out of my depth, I was not able to work. In
this necessity, I was forced to swim behind, and push the boat forwards as
often as I could, with one of my hands; and the tide favouring me, I advanced

so far, that I could just hold up my chin and feel the ground. I rested two or
three minutes, and then gave the boat another shove, and so on till the sea was
no higher than my armpits. And now the most laborious part being over, I
took out my other cables which were stowed in one of the ships, and fastening
them first to the boat, and then to nine of the vessels which attended me; the
wind being favourable, the seamen towed, and I shoved till we arrived within
forty yards of the shore; and waiting till the tide was out, I got dry to the boat,
and by the assistance of two thousand men, with ropes and engines, I made a
shift to turn it on its bottom, and found it was but little damaged.

I shall not trouble the reader with the difficulties I was under by the help of
certain paddles, which cost me ten days making, to get my boat to the royal

COMMENTARY
Gulliver describes how he rescues the boat by first pushing it toward shore and
then tugging it with ropes. He is relieved to find it is in good condition.

port of Blefuscu; where a mighty concourse of people appeared upon my arrival, full of wonder at the sight of so prodigious a vessel. I told the Emperor, that my good fortune had thrown this boat in my way, to carry me to some place from whence I might return into my native country; and begged his majesty's orders for getting materials to fit it up; together with his licence to depart; which, after some kind expostulations, he was pleased to grant.

I did very much wonder, in all this time, not to have heard of any express relating to me from our Emperor to the court of Blefuscu. But I was afterwards given privately to understand, that his imperial majesty, never imagining I had the least notice of his designs, believed I was only gone to Blefuscu in performance of my promise, according to the licence he had given me, which was well known at our court; and would return in a few days when that ceremony was ended. But he was at last in pain at my long absence; and, after consulting with the treasurer, and the rest of that cabal, a person of quality was dispatched with the copy of the articles against me. This envoy had instructions to represent to the monarch of Blefuscu, the great lenity of his master, who was content to punish me no further than with the loss of mine eyes: that I had fled from justice, and if I did not return in two hours, I should be deprived of my title of *Nardac*, and declared a traitor. The envoy further added; that in order to maintain the peace and amity between both Empires, his master expected, that his brother of Blefuscu would give orders to have me sent back to Lilliput, bound hand and foot, to be punished as a traitor.

The Emperor of Blefuscu having taken three days to consult, returned an answer consisting of many civilities and excuses. He said, that as for sending me bound, his brother knew it was impossible; that although I had deprived him of his fleet, yet he owed great obligations to me for many good offices I had done him in making the peace. That however, both their majesties would soon be made easy; for I had found a prodigious vessel on the shore, able to carry me on the sea, which he had given order to fit up with my own assistance and direction; and he hoped in a few weeks both Empires would be freed from so insupportable an incumbrance.

COMMENTARY

Gulliver receives the emperor of Blefuscu's permission to set to sea to make his return to England. The Lilliputian emperor sends a message to the emperor of Blefuscu informing him of Gulliver's "treason" and demanding that Gulliver be returned to them. The emperor of Blefuscu replies by saying that Gulliver will soon be leaving the islands altogether, which would solve their disagreement.

concourse: crowd
expostulations: attempts to dissuade me
cabal: group of plotters
amity: friendship
offices: actions
incumbrance: burden

With this answer the envoy returned to Lilliput, and the monarch of Blefuscu related to me all that had past; offering me at the same time (but under the strictest confidence) his gracious protection, if I would continue in his service; wherein although I believed him sincere, yet I resolved never more to put any confidence in princes or ministers, where I could possibly avoid it; and therefore, with all due acknowledgements for his favourable intentions, I humbly begged to be excused. I told him that since fortune, whether good or evil, had thrown a vessel in my way; I was resolved to venture myself in the ocean, rather than be an occasion of difference between two such mighty monarchs. Neither did I find the Emperor at all displeased; and I discovered by a certain accident, that he was very glad of my resolution, and so were most of his ministers.

These considerations moved me to hasten my departure somewhat sooner than I intended; to which the court, impatient to have me gone, very readily contributed. Five hundred workmen were employed to make two sails to my boat, according to my directions, by quilting thirteen fold of their strongest linen together. I was at the pains of making ropes and cables, by twisting ten, twenty or thirty of the thickest and strongest of theirs. A great stone that I happened to find, after a long search by the seashore, served me for an anchor. I had the tallow of three hundred cows for greasing my boat, and other uses. I was at incredible pains in cutting down some of the largest timber trees for oars and masts, wherein I was, however, much assisted by his majesty's ship-carpenters, who helped me in smoothing them, after I had done the rough work.

In about a month, when all was prepared, I sent to receive his majesty's commands, and to take my leave. The Emperor and royal family came out of the palace: I lay down on my face to kiss his hand, which he very graciously gave me; so did the Empress, and young princes of the blood. His majesty presented me with fifty purses of two hundred *sprugs* apiece, together with his picture at full length, which I put immediately into one of my gloves, to keep it from being hurt. The ceremonies at my departure were too many to trouble the reader with at this time.

tallow: fat

COMMENTARY

The emperor of Blefuscu promises to protect Gulliver, but while thanking him for his help, Gulliver decides that he has begun to distrust rulers. The Blefuscudians are happy for Gulliver to go, and after he has prepared for the voyage, he takes his leave.

I stored the boat with the carcasses of an hundred oxen, and three hundred sheep, with bread and drink proportionable, and as much meat ready dressed as four hundred cooks could provide. I took with me six cows and two bulls alive, with as many yews and rams, intending to carry them into my own country, and propagate the breed. And to feed them on board, I had a good bundle of hay, and a bag of corn. I would gladly have taken a dozen of the natives; but this was a thing the Emperor would by no means permit; and besides a diligent search into my pockets, his majesty engaged my honour not to carry away any of his subjects, although with their own consent and desire.

FAST FORWARD: to page 83

Having thus prepared all things as well as I was able, I set sail on the twenty-fourth day of September 1701, at six in the morning; and when I had gone about four leagues to the northward, the wind being at south-east; at six

COMMENTARY
Gulliver takes some cattle and sheep, which he intends to breed in England. He is not allowed, however, to take any of the people of Blefuscu. The beginning of his journey is described.

proportionable: in proportion
propagate: reproduce

in the evening, I descried a small island about half a league to the north-west.
I advanced forward, and cast anchor on the lee-side of the island, which
seemed to be inhabited. I then took some refreshment, and went to my rest.
I slept well, and as I conjecture at least six hours; for I found the day broke in
two hours after I awaked. It was a clear night. I ate my breakfast before the
sun was up; and heaving anchor, the wind being favourable, I steered the same
course that I had done the day before, wherein I was directed by my pocket-
compass. My intention was to reach, if possible, one of those islands, which I
had reason to believe lay to north-east of Van Diemen's Land. I discovered
nothing all that day; but upon the next, about three in the afternoon, when I
had by my computation made twenty-four leagues from Blefuscu, I descried a
sail steering to the south-east; my course was due east. I hailed her, but could
get no answer; yet I found I gained upon her, for the wind slackened. I made
all the sail I could, and in half an hour she spyed me, then hung out her
antient, and discharged a gun. It is not easy to express the joy I was in upon
the unexpected hope of once more seeing my beloved country, and the dear
pledges I had left in it. The ship slackened her sails, and I came up with her
between five and six in the evening, September 26; but my heart leapt within
me to see her English colours. I put my cows and sheep into my coat-pockets,
and got on board with all my little cargo of provisions. The vessel was an
English merchantman, returning from Japan by the North and South Seas; the
captain, Mr John Biddel of Deptford, a very civil man, and an excellent sailor.
We were now in the latitude of 30 degrees south; there were about fifty men in
the ship; and here I met an old comrade of mine, one Peter Williams, who gave
me a good character to the captain. This gentleman treated me with kindness,
and desired I would let him know what place I came from last, and whither I
was bound; which I did in few words; but he thought I was raving, and that
the dangers I underwent had disturbed my head; whereupon I took my black
cattle and sheep out of my pocket, which, after great astonishment, clearly
convinced him of my veracity. I then showed him the gold given me by the
Emperor of Blefuscu, together with his majesty's picture at full length, and

descried: saw
lee-side: sheltered side
antient: flag
pledges: obligations i.e., family
gave me a good character: spoke well of
  me
veracity: truthfulness

COMMENTARY
Gulliver lands on an island, rests, and
then sets sail again. Eventually he is
picked up by an English ship. The
captain does not believe his story until
he is shown the tiny cattle and sheep.

some other rarities of that country. I gave him two purses of two hundred sprugs each, and promised, when we arrived in England, to make him a present of a cow and a sheep big with young.

I shall not trouble the reader with a particular account of this voyage, which was very prosperous for the most part. We arrived in the Downs on the 13th of April 1702. I had only one misfortune, that the rats on board carried away one of my sheep; I found her bones in a hole, picked clean from the flesh. The rest of my cattle I got safe on shore, and set them a grazing in a bowling-green at Greenwich, where the fineness of the grass made them feed very heartily, although I had always feared the contrary: neither could I possibly have preserved them in so long a voyage, if the captain had not allowed me some of his best biscuit, which rubbed to powder, and mingled with water, was their constant food. The short time I continued in England, I made a considerable profit by showing my cattle to many persons of quality, and others: and before I began my second voyage, I sold them for six hundred pounds. Since my last return, I find the breed is considerably increased, especially the sheep; which I hope will prove much to the advantage of the woolen manufacture, by the fineness of the fleeces. ◀◀

I stayed but two months with my wife and family; for my insatiable desire of seeing foreign countries would suffer me to continue no longer. I left fifteen hundred pounds with my wife, and fixed her in a good house in Redriff. My remaining stock I carried with me, part in money, and part in goods, in hopes to improve my fortunes. My eldest uncle, John, had left me an estate in land, near Epping, of about thirty pounds a year; and I had a long lease of the Black

---

REWIND: . . . of the fleeces.
Gulliver describes his journey back to England. After setting sail in his boat he is eventually picked up by an English ship and taken home. He also explains that he managed to keep some of his Lilliputian sheep and cattle alive and has now sold them in England.

COMMENTARY
The journey back to England is safe except that one of the sheep is eaten by rats. Back in England, Gulliver shows his cattle and sheep for profit and then sells them. However, after only two months Gulliver feels a strong desire to travel again.

big with young: which were pregnant
insatiable desire: constant urge

Bull in Fetter Lane, which yielded me as much more: so that I was not in any
danger of leaving my family upon the parish. My son Johnny, named so after
his uncle, was at the grammar school, and a towardly child. My daughter
Betty (who is now well married, and has children) was then at her needlework.
I took leave of my wife, and boy and girl, with tears on both sides, and went
on board the *Adventure*, a merchant-ship of three hundred tons, bound for
Surat, Captain John Nicholas of Liverpool, commander. But my account of
this voyage must be referred to the second part of my travels.

THE END OF THE FIRST PART

upon the parish: in need of charity
towardly: dutiful
Surat: an Indian port
be referred to: wait until

COMMENTARY
Gulliver makes sure that all his family is
provided for before setting out on
another journey in a ship called the
Adventure.

PART TWO
A VOYAGE TO BROBDINGNAG

1

Look out for . . .
- what this chapter reveals about Gulliver when he is faced with a number of dangerous situations.
- Gulliver's views on the way in which we judge people's looks.

A great storm described. The long boat sent to fetch water, the author goes with it to discover the country. He is left on shore, is seized by one of the natives, and carried to a farmer's house. His reception there, with several accidents that happened there. A description of the inhabitants.

FAST FORWARD: to page 88

Having been condemned by nature and fortune to an active and restless life; in two months after my return, I again left my native country, and took shipping in the Downs on the 20th day of June 1702, in the *Adventure*, Capt. John Nicholas, a Cornish man, commander, bound for Surat. We had a very prosperous gale till we arrived at the Cape of Good Hope, where we landed for fresh water, but discovering a leak we unshipped our goods, and

nature and fortune: my natural desires and fate
prosperous gale: helpful wind

COMMENTARY
Gulliver sets out on his voyage and reaches South Africa.

wintered there; for the captain falling sick of the ague, we could not leave the Cape till the end of March. We then set sail, and had a good voyage till we passed the Streights of Madagascar; but having got northward of that island, and to about five degrees south latitude, the winds, which in those seas are observed to blow a constant equal gale between the north and west, from the beginning of December to the beginning of May, on the 19th of April began to blow with much greater violence, and more westerly than usual, continuing so for twenty days together, during which time we were driven a little to the east of the Molucca islands, and about three degrees northward of the line, as our captain found by an observation he took the 2nd of May, at which time the wind ceased, and it was a perfect calm, whereat I was not a little rejoyced. But he being a man well experienced in the navigation of those seas, bid us all prepared against a storm, which accordingly happened the day following: for a southern wind, called the southern *monsoon*, began to set in.

Finding it was like to overblow, we took in our spitsail, and stood by to hand the foresail; but making foul weather, we looked the guns were all fast, and handed the mizen. The ship lay very broad off, so we thought it better spooning before the sea, than trying or hulling. We reefed the foresail and set him, we hauled aft the fore-sheet; the helm was hard a weather. The ship wore bravely. We belayed the foredown-hall; but the sail was split, and we hauled down the yard, and got the sail into the ship, and unbound all the things clear of it. It was a very fierce storm; the sea broke strange and dangerous. We hauled off upon the lanyard of the whipstaff, and helped the man at helm. We would not get down our top-mast, but let all stand, because she scudded before the sea very well, and we knew that the top-mast being aloft, the ship was the wholesomer, and made better way through the sea, seeing we had sea room. When the storm was over, we set foresail and mainsail, and brought the ship to. Then we set the mizen, maintop-sail and the foretop-sail. Our course was east-north-east, the wind was at south-west. We got the starboard tacks aboard, we cast off our weather-braces and lifts; we set in the lee-braces, and hauled forward by the weather-bowlings, and hauled them tight, and belayed

COMMENTARY

The *Adventure* travels for a few months before a ferocious storm begins and blows the ship off course. During the description of the storm, Gulliver shows his sailing knowledge. Swift put this passage in to laugh at the way some people like to show off by using a lot of technical words. A group of technical words associated with a set of people (such as sailors, lawyers, politicians, computer operators, etc.) is often called *jargon*.

ague: fever

line, overblow, spitsail, foresail, mizen, spooning, trying, hulling, reefed, fore-sheet, helm, belayed, foredown-hall, yard, lanyard, whipstaff, top-mast, scudded, mainsail, starboard tacks, weather-braces and lifts, lee-braces, weather-bowlings: all sailing terms

them, and hauled over the mizen tack to windward, and kept her full and by as near as she would lie.

During this storm, which was followed by a strong wind west-south-west, we were carried by my computation about five hundred leagues to the east, so that the oldest sailor on board could not tell in what part of the world we were. Our provisions held out well, our ship was staunch, and our crew all in good health; but we lay in the utmost distress for water. We thought it best to hold on the same course rather than turn more northerly, which might have brought us to the north-west parts of the great Tartary and into the frozen sea.

On the 16th day of June 1703, a boy on the topmast discovered land. On the 17th we came in full view of a great island or continent (for we knew not whether), on the south-side whereof was a small neck of land jutting out into the sea, and a creek too shallow to hold a ship of above one hundred tuns. We cast anchor within a league of this creek, and our captain sent a dozen of his men well armed in the long board, with vessels for water if any could be found. I desired his leave to go with them, that I might see the country, and make what discoveries I could. When we came to land we saw no river or spring, nor any sign of inhabitants. Our men therefore wandered on the shore to find out some fresh water near the sea, and I walked alone about a mile on the other side, where I observed the country all barren and rocky. I now began to be weary, and seeing nothing to entertain my curiosity, I returned gently down towards the creek; and the sea being full in my view, I saw our men already got into the boat, and rowing for life to the ship. I was going to hollow after them although it had been to little purpose, when I observed a huge creature walking after them in the sea, as fast as he could: he waded not much deeper than his knees, and took prodigious strides: but our men had the start of him

---

REWIND: . . . the frozen sea.
Gulliver describes how he set out on another voyage and how the ship was blown off course because of a storm.

---

staunch: strong
Tartary: large region in Central Asia during Gulliver's time
whether: which of the two
hollow: shout

COMMENTARY
A storm carries them off course. The ship eventually arrives at land with the crew in desperate need of water. A dozen get into a small boat and row ashore. Gulliver wanders off to explore the coastline. On returning, he sees the crew rowing back to the ship chased by a giant man.

half a league, and the sea thereabouts being full of sharp pointed rocks, the monster was not able to overtake the boat. This I was afterwards told, for I durst not stay to see the issue of that adventure; but ran as fast as I could the way I first went; and then climbed up a steep hill, which gave me some prospect of the country. I found it fully cultivated; but that which first surprised me was the length of the grass, which is those grounds that seemed to be kept for hay, was above twenty foot high.

I fell into a high road, for so I took it to be, although it served to the inhabitants only as a foot path through a field of barley. Here I walked on for some time, but could see little on either side, it being now near harvest, and the corn rising at least forty foot. I was an hour walking to the end of this field; which was fenced in with a hedge of at least one hundred and twenty foot high, and the trees so lofty that I could make no computation of their altitude. There was a stile to pass from the field into the next: it had four steps, and a stone to cross over when you came to the uppermost. It was impossible for me to climb this stile, because every step was six foot high, and the upper stone above twenty. I was endeavouring to find some gap in the hedge; when I discovered one of the inhabitants in the next field advancing towards the stile, of the same size with him whom I saw in the sea pursuing

COMMENTARY
The crew escape from the giant, but Gulliver is now stranded and flees into the nearby fields where everything seems to be twelve times larger than in England. Gulliver comes to a massive stile, and as he tries to get over it, he sees another giant, a huge farmworker.

issue: outcome
prospect: view
altitude: height
uppermost: top one

our boat. He appeared as tall as an ordinary spire-steeple; and took about ten yards at every stride, as near as I could guess. I was struck with the utmost fear and astonishment, and ran to hide myself in the corn, from whence I saw him at the top of the stile, looking back into the next field on the right hand; and heard him call in a voice many degrees louder than a speaking-trumpet; but the noise was so high in the air, that at first I certainly thought it was thunder. Whereupon seven monsters like himself came towards him with reaping-hooks in their hands, each hook about the largeness of six scythes. These people were not so well clad as the first, whose servants or labourers they seemed to be. For, upon some words he spoke, they went to reap the corn in the field where I lay. I kept from them at as great a distance as I could, but was forced to move with extreme difficulty; for the stalks of corn were sometimes not above a foot distant, so that I could hardly squeeze my body betwixt them. However, I made a shift to go forward till I came to a part of the field where the corn had been laid by the rain and wind: here it was impossible for me to advance a step; for the stalks were so interwoven that I could not creep through, and the beards of the fallen ears so strong and pointed, that they pierced through my clothes into my flesh. At the same time I heard the reapers not above an hundred yards behind me. Being quite dispirited with toil, and wholly overcome by grief and despair, I lay down between two ridges, and heartily wished I might there end my days. I bemoaned my desolate widow, and fatherless children: I lamented my own folly and wilfulness in attempting a second voyage against the advice of all my friends and relations. In this terrible agitation of mind I could not forbear thinking of Lilliput, whose inhabitants looked upon me as the greatest prodigy that ever appeared in the world; where I was able to draw an imperial fleet in my hand, and perform those other actions which will be recorded for ever in the chronicles of that Empire, while posterity shall hardly believe them, although attested by millions. I reflected with a mortification it must prove to me to appear as inconsiderable in this nation, as one single Lilliputian would be among us. But, this I conceived was to be the least of my misfortunes: for, as human creatures are observed to be

spire-steeple: the pointed structure
    on top of a church tower
speaking-trumpet: instrument like a
    megaphone
scythes: tools for cutting corn,
    having a sharp blade and a long
    handle
distant: apart
betwixt: between
dispirited with toil: made weary by
    hard work
forbear: help
attested: witnessed
mortification: humiliation
inconsiderable: tiny

COMMENTARY
Gulliver runs into the corn to hide but eventually comes to a place where the corn is so thick that he cannot get through. He lies down in misery, prepared to die. While lying down, Gulliver realizes that compared to the giants he is like a Lilliputian.

more savage and cruel in proportion to their bulk; what could I expect but to be a morsel in the mouth of the first among these enormous barbarians who should happen to seize me? Undoubtedly philosophers are in the right when they tell us, that nothing is great or little otherwise than by comparison: it might have pleased fortune to let the Lilliputians find some nation, where the people were as diminutive with respect to them, as they were to me. And who knows but that even this prodigious race of mortals might be equally overmatched in some distant part of the world, whereof we have yet no discovery?

Scared and confounded as I was, I could not forbear going on with these reflections; when one of the reapers approaching within ten yards of the ridge where I lay, made me apprehend that with the next step I should be squashed to death under his foot, or cut in two with his reaping hook. And therefore when he was again above to move, I screamed as loud as fear could make me. Whereupon the huge creature trod short, and looking round about under him for some time, at last espied me as I lay on the ground. He considered a while with the caution of one who endeavours to lay hold on a small dangerous animal in such a manner that it shall not be able to either to scratch or to bite him; as I myself have sometimes done with a weasel in England. At length he ventured to take me up behind by the middle between his forefinger and thumb, and brought me within three yards of his eyes, that he might

COMMENTARY
Gulliver worries that the bigger someone is the more brutal he or she can be and fears that these giants could be very brutal indeed. He imagines that there may be other races in the world that are even bigger than these giants and some that are smaller than the Lilliputians. As he is thinking these things he is almost trodden on by one of the giants but manages to scream out in time. The giant picks Gulliver up and examines him.

diminutive: small
with respect: compared

behold my shape more perfectly. I guessed this meaning; and my good fortune gave me so much presence of mind, that I resolved not to struggle in the least as he held me in the air above sixty foot from the ground; although he grievously pinched my sides, for fear I should slip through his fingers. All I ventured was to raise mine eyes towards the sun, and place my hands together in a supplicating posture, and to speak some words in an humble melancholy tone, suitable to the condition I then was in. For I apprehended every moment that he would dash me against the ground, as we usually do any little hateful animal which we have a mind to destroy. But my good star would have it, that he appeared pleased with my voice and gestures, and began to look upon me as a curiosity, much wondering to hear me pronounce articulate words, although he could not understand them. In the meantime I was not able to forbear groaning and shedding tears, and turning my head towards my sides; letting him know, as well as I could, how cruelly I was hurt by the pressure of his thumb and finger. He seemed to apprehend my meaning; for, lifting up the lappet of his coat, he put me gently into it and immediately ran along with me to his master, who was a substantial farmer, and the same person I had first seen in the field.

The farmer having (as I supposed by their talk) received such an account of me as his servant could give him, took a piece of a small straw, about the size of a walking staff, and therewith lifted up the lappets of my coat; which it seems he thought to be some kind of covering that nature had given me. He blew my hairs aside to take a better view of my face. He called his hinds about him, and asked them (as I afterwards learned) whether they had ever seen in the fields any little creature that resembled me. He then placed me softly on the ground upon all four, but I got immediately up, and walked slowly backwards and forwards, to let those people see I had no intent to run away. They all sate down in a circle about me, the better to observe my motions. I pulled off my hat, and made a low bow towards the farmer: I fell on my knees, and lifted up my hands and eyes, and spoke several words as loud as I could: I took a purse of gold out of my pocket, and humbly presented it to him. He

behold my shape more perfectly: see me
more clearly
grievously: painfully
supplicating: pleading
melancholy: sad
pronounce articulate words: speak in a clear
language
lappet: flap of a coat
substantial farmer: farmer with a large
amount of property
walking staff: walking stick
hinds: farmworkers

COMMENTARY
Gulliver tries to communicate through gestures that he wants to be shown mercy. The farmworker is amused by Gulliver who appears as a little animal to him. He is then taken to the farmer for inspection and is surrounded by a group of farmworkers who examine him.

received it on the palm of his hand, then applied it close to his eye, to see what it was, and afterwards turned it several times with the point of a pin (which he took out of his sleeve), but could make nothing of it. Whereupon I made a sign that he should place his hand on the ground: I then took the purse, and opening it, poured all the gold into his palm. There were six Spanish pieces of four pistoles each, besides twenty or thirty smaller coins. I saw him wet the tip of his little finger upon his tongue, and take up one of my largest pieces, and then another; but he seemed to be wholly ignorant what they were. He made a sign to put them again into my purse, and the purse again into my pocket; which after offering to him several times, I thought it best to do.

The farmer by this time was convinced I must be a rational creature. He spoke often to me, but the sound of his voice pierced my ears like that of a watermill; yet his words were articulate enough. I answered as loud as I could in several languages; and he often laid his ear within two yards of me, but all in vain, for we were wholly unintelligible to each other. He then sent his servants to their work, and taking his handkerchief out of his pocket, he doubled and spread it on his hand, which he placed flat on the ground with the palm upwards, making me a sign to step into it, as I could easily do, for it was not above a foot in thickness. I thought it my part to obey; and for fear of falling, laid myself at full length upon the handkerchief, with the remainder of which he lapped me up to the head for further security; and in this manner carried me home to his house. There he called his wife, and showed me to her; but she screamed and ran back as women in England do at the sight of a toad or a spider. However, when she had a while seen my behaviour, and how well I observed the signs her husband made, she was soon reconciled, and by degrees grew extreamly tender of me.

It was about twelve at noon, and the servant brought in dinner. It was only one substantial dish of meat (fit for the plain condition of an husbandman) in a dish of about four and twenty foot diameter. The company were the farmer and his wife, three children, and an old grandmother: when they were sat down, the farmer placed me at some distance from him on the table, which

COMMENTARY

Gulliver offers the giants some money, hoping that this will make them treat him with mercy. However, the coins are so small to them that they do not recognize them and return the money to Gulliver. As in Lilliput, the conversations are all through gestures as the giants and Gulliver speak different languages. Gulliver is taken home by the farmer in a handkerchief. At first, the farmer's wife dislikes Gulliver, thinking of him as a creature like a spider. However, she soon grows fond of him.

pistoles: gold currency
unintelligible: unable to understand
lapped: wrapped
husbandman: farmer

was thirty foot high from the floor. I was in a terrible fright, and kept as far as I could from the edge for fear of falling. The wife minced a bit of meat, then crumbed some bread on a trencher, and placed it before me. I made her a low bow, took out my knife and fork, and fell to eat, which gave them exceeding delight. The mistress sent her maid for a small dram-cup, which held about two gallons, and filled it with drink: I took up the vessel with much difficulty in both hands, and in a most respectful manner drank to her ladyship's health, expressing the words as loud as I could in English; which made the company laugh so heartily, that I was almost deafened with the noise. This liquor tasted like a small cider, and was not unpleasant. Then the master made me a sign to come to his trencher side; but as I walked on the table, being in great surprise all the time, as the indulgent reader will easily conceive and excuse, I happened to stumble against a crust, and fell flat on my face, but received no hurt. I got up immediately, and observing the good people to be in much

concern, I took my hat (which I held under my arm out of good manners) and waving it over my head, made three huzzas, to show I had got no mischief by the fall. But advancing forwards toward my master (as I shall henceforth call him) his youngest son who sat next to him, an arch boy of about ten years old, took me up by the legs, and held me so high in the air, that I trembled every limb; but his father snatched me from him; and at the same time gave him such a box on the left ear, as would have felled an European troop of horse to the earth; ordering him to be taken from

dram-cup: small cup
huzzas: cheers
arch: mischievous
troop of horse: section of the cavalry

COMMENTARY
Gulliver is fed at the giant table and is amazed at the vast quantities of food that the giants eat. While at the table the son of the farmer playfully picks Gulliver up and holds him upside down.

the table. But, being afraid the boy might owe me a spite; and well remembering how mischievous all children among us naturally are to sparrows, rabbits, young kittens, and puppy dogs, I fell on my knees, and pointing to the boy, made my master understand, as well as I could, that I desired his son might be pardoned. The father complied, and the lad took his seat again; whereupon I went to him and kissed his hand, which my master took, and made him stroke me gently with it.

In the midst of dinner my mistress's favourite cat leapt into her lap. I heard a noise behind me like that of a dozen stocking-weavers at work; and turning my head, I found it proceeded from the purring of this animal, who seemed to be three times larger than an ox, as I computed by the view of her head, and one of her paws, while her mistress was feeding and stroking her. The fierceness of this creature's countenance altogether discomposed me; although I stood at the further end of the table, above fifty foot off; and although my mistress held her fast for fear she might give a spring, and seize me in her talons. But it happened there was no danger; for the cat took not the least notice of me when my master placed me within three yards of her. And as I have been always told, and found true by experience in my travels, that flying, or discovering fear before a fierce animal, is a certain way to make it pursue or attack you; so I resolved in this dangerous juncture to show no manner of concern. I walked with intrepidity five or six times before the very head of the cat, and came within half a yard of her; whereupon she drew herself back, as if she were more afraid of me: I had less apprehension concerning the dogs, whereof three or four came into the room, as it is usual in farmers houses; one of which was a mastiff equal in bulk to four elephants, and a greyhound somewhat taller than the mastiff, but not so large.

When dinner was almost done, the nurse came in with a child of a year old in her arms; who immediately spied me, and began a squall that you might have heard from London Bridge to Chelsea, after the usual oratory of infants, to get me for a plaything. The mother out of pure indulgence took me up, and put me towards the child, who presently seized me by the middle, and got my

COMMENTARY

The son is punished for playing with Gulliver, but Gulliver is smart enough to show that he forgives the son as he does not want him to become an enemy. Gulliver sees the cats and dogs of the household, all of whom are many times bigger than English ones.

complied: agreed
juncture: moment
intrepidity: fearlessness
mastiff: large, powerful dog
squall: wail
oratory: way of speaking

head in his mouth, where I roared so loud that the urchin was frighted, and let me drop, and I should infallibly have broke my neck, if the mother had not held her apron under me. The nurse to quiet her babe made use of a rattle, which was a kind of hollow vessel filled with great stones, and fastened by a cable to the child's waist: but all in vain so that she was forced to apply the last remedy by giving it suck. I must confess no object ever disgusted me so much as the sight of her monstrous breast, which I cannot tell what to compare with, so as to give the curious reader an idea of its bulk, shape and colour. It stood prominent six foot, and could not be less than sixteen in circumference. The nipple was about half the bigness of my head, and the hue both of that and the dug so varified with spots, pimples and freckles, that nothing could appear more nauseous: for I had a near sight of her, she sitting down the more conveniently to give suck, and I standing on the table. This made me reflect upon the fair skins of our English ladies, who appear so beautiful to us, only because they are of our own size, and their defects not to be seen but through a magnifying glass, where we find by experiment that the smoothest and whitest skins look rough and coarse, and ill coloured.

COMMENTARY

The baby of the family, who is still very large compared to Gulliver, picks him up and puts him in its mouth. He screams and the baby drops him in fright. Fortunately, Gulliver is caught in the mother's apron before he hits the floor. The mother then breast-feeds the baby and Gulliver describes how horrible the gigantic breast seems. However, he says this is just because of its difference in size. English people's skin would appear as marked and hairy if put under a magnifying glass.

urchin: small child
dug: breast

I remember when I was at Lilliput, the complexions of those diminutive people appeared to me the fairest in the world: and talking upon this subject with a person of learning there, who was an intimate friend of mine; he said, that my face appeared much fairer and smoother when he looked on me from the ground, than it did upon a nearer view when I took him up in my hand, and brought him close, which he confessed was at first a very shocking sight. He said, he could discover great holes in my skin, that the stumps of my beard were ten times stronger than the bristles of a boar, and my complexion made up of several colours altogether disagreeable: although I must beg leave to say for myself, that I am as fair as most of my sex and country, and very little sunburnt by all my travels. On the other side, discoursing of the ladies in that Emperor's court, he used to tell me, one had freckles, another too wide a mouth, a third too large a nose, nothing of which I was able to distinguish. I confess this reflection was obvious enough; which, however, I could not forbear, lest the reader might think those vast creatures were actually deformed: for I must do them justice to say they are a comely race of people; and particularly the features of my master's countenance, although he were but a farmer, when I beheld him from the height of sixty foot, appeared very well proportioned.

When dinner was done, my master went out to his labourers; and as I could discover by his voice and gesture, gave his wife a strict charge to take care of me. I was very much tired and disposed to sleep, which my mistress perceiving, she put me on her own bed, and covered me with a clean white handkerchief, but larger and coarser than the main sail of a man of war.

I slept about two hours, and dreamed I was at home with my wife and children, which aggravated my sorrows when I awaked and found myself alone in a vast room, between two and three hundred foot wide, and above two hundred high, lying in a bed twenty yards wide. My mistress was gone about her household affairs, and had locked me in. The bed was eight yards from the floor. Some natural necessities required me to get down: I durst not presume to call, and if I had, it would have been in vain with such a voice as mine at so

COMMENTARY
Gulliver remembers that his skin appeared ugly to the Lilliputians, whereas theirs appeared perfect. He decides that ugliness or beauty depends on the point of view you are looking from and that the giants are not really ugly at all. Later, Gulliver feels tired and goes to sleep underneath one of the giant's handkerchiefs.

beg leave: ask
discoursing of: discussing
comely: handsome
natural necessities: need to go to the bathroom

great a distance from the room where I lay, to the kitchen where the family kept. While I was under these circumstances, two rats crept up the curtains, and ran smelling backwards and forwards on the bed: one of them came up almost to my face; whereupon I rose in a fright, and drew out my hanger to defend myself. These horrible animals had the boldness to attack me on both sides, and one of them held his fore-feet at my collar; but I had the good fortune to rip up his belly before he could do me any mischief. He fell down at my feet; and the other seeing the fate of his comrade, made his escape, but not

without one good wound on the back, which I gave him as he fled, and made the blood run trickling from him. After this exploit I walked gently to and fro on the bed, to recover my breath and loss of spirits. These creatures were of the size of a large mastiff, but infinitely more nimble and fierce, so that if I had taken off my belt before I went to sleep, I must have infallibly been torn to pieces and devoured. I measured the tail of the dead rat, and found it to be two yards long, wanting an inch; but it went against my stomach to drag the carcass off the bed, where it lay still bleeding; I observed it had yet some life, but with a strong slash cross the neck, I thoroughly dispatched it.

hanger: sword
dispatched: killed

COMMENTARY
When Gulliver wakes up he is attacked by two giant rats the size of large dogs. He shows his bravery by fighting them off with his sword.

Soon after, my mistress came into the room, who seeing me all bloody, ran and took me up in her hand. I pointed to the dead rat, smiling and making other signs to show I was not hurt; whereat she was extremely rejoiced, calling the maid to take up the dead rat with a pair of tongs, and throw it out of the window. Then she set me on a table, where I showed her my hanger all bloody, and wiping it on the lappet of my coat, returned it to the scabbard. I was pressed to do more than one thing, which another could no do for me; and therefore endeavoured to make my mistress understand that I desired to be set down on the floor; which after she had done, my bashfulness would not suffer me to express myself farther than by pointing to the door, and bowing several times. The good woman with much difficulty at last perceived what I would be at; and taking me up again in her hand, walked into the garden where she set me down. I went on one side about two hundred yards, and beckoning to her not to look or to follow me, I hid myself between two leaves of sorrel, and there discharged the necessities of nature.

I hope the gentle reader will excuse me for dwelling on these and the like particulars, which however insignificant they may appear to grovelling vulgar minds, yet will certainly help a philosopher to enlarge his thoughts and imagination, and apply them to the benefit of public as well as private life, which was my sole design in presenting this and other accounts of my travels to the world; wherein I have been chiefly studious of truth, without affecting any ornaments of learning or of style. But the whole scene of this voyage made so strong an impression on my mind, and is so deeply fixed in my memory, that in committing it to paper, I did not omit one material circumstance: however, upon a strict review, I blotted out several passages of less moment which were in my first copy, for fear of being censured as tedious and trifling, whereof travellers are often, perhaps not without justice, accused.

COMMENTARY

Gulliver needs to go to the bathroom and manages to explain to the farmer's wife that he wants to find a private spot outside. He tells his readers that he is writing so that people can learn from his travels. He has attempted to write in a simple style and has tried to cut out anything that he feels is irrelevant.

sorrel: a plant

without affecting any ornaments of learning or of style: without showing off my learning or pretending to write with style

material circumstance: important event

censured: condemned

2

A description of the farmer's daughter. The author carried to a market-town, and then to the metropolis. The particulars of his journey.

My mistress had a daughter of nine years old, a child of forward parts for her age, very dexterous at her needle, and skilful in dressing her baby. Her mother and she contrived to fit up the baby's cradle for me against night: the cradle was put into a small drawer of a cabinet, and the drawer placed upon a hanging shelf for fear of the rats. This was my bed all the time I stayed with those people, although made more convenient by degrees, as I began to learn their language, and make my wants known. This young girl was so handy, that after I had once or twice pulled off my clothes before her, she was able to dress and undress me, although I never gave her that trouble when she would let me do either myself. She made me seven shirts, and some other linnen of as fine cloth as could be got, which indeed was coarser than sackcloth; and these she constantly washed for me with her own hands. She was likewise my school-mistress to teach me the language: when I pointed to

particulars: details
of forward parts: advanced
dexterous: skillful
baby: doll

COMMENTARY
Gulliver is looked after by the farmer's daughter who provides a doll's cradle for Gulliver to sleep in. This is placed high up so as to keep him safe from rats. The farmer's daughter makes clothes for him and teaches him the language of the land.

any thing, she told me the name of it in her own tongue, so that in a few days
I was able to call for whatever I had a mind to. She was very good natured,
and not above forty foot high, being little for her age. She gave me the name
of *Grildrig*, which the family took up, and afterwards the whole kingdom. The
word imports what the Latins call *nanunculus*, the Italians *homunceletino*, and
the English mannikin. To her I chiefly owe my preservation in that country:
we never parted while I was there; I called her my *Glumdalclitch*, or little nurse:
and I should be guilty of great ingratitude if I omitted this honourable
mention of her care and affection towards me, which I heartily wish it lay in
my power to requite as she deserves, instead of being the innocent but
unhappy instrument of her disgrace, as I have too much reason to fear.

It now began to be known and talked of in the neighbourhood, that my
master had found a strange animal in the field, but the bigness of a *splacknuck*,
but exactly shaped in every part like a human creature; which it likewise
imitated in all its actions; seemed to speak in a little language of its own, had
already learned several words of theirs, went erect upon two legs, was tame
and gentle, would come when it was called, do whatever it was bid, had the
finest limbs in the world, and a complexion fairer than a nobleman's daughter
of three years old. Another farmer who lived hard by, and was a particular
friend of my master, came on a visit on purpose to enquire into the truth of
this story. I was immediately produced, and placed upon a table; where I
walked as I was commanded, drew my hanger, put it up again, made my
reverence to my master's guest, asked him in his own language how he did,
and told him he was welcome, just as my little nurse had instructed me. This
man, who was old and dim-sighted, put on his spectacles to behold me better,
at which I could not forbear laughing very heartily, for his eyes appeared like
the full moon shining into a chamber at two windows. Our people, who
discovered the cause of my mirth, bore me company in laughing, at which the
old fellow was fool enough to be angry and out of countenance. He had the
character of a great miser, and to my misfortune he well deserved it by the
cursed advice he gave my master, to show me as a sight upon a market-day in

COMMENTARY
Gulliver calls the farmer's daughter
"Glumdalclitch," which is Brobdingnagian
for "little nurse." He becomes very
fond of her. News gets out that a tiny
manlike creature (Gulliver) has been
found. Lots of visitors want to see
Gulliver, one of whom suggests that
the farmer takes him to market and
puts him on display for profit.

mannikin: dwarf   *instrument*: cause
requite: reward   *reverence*: bow

the next town, which was half an hour's riding, about two and twenty miles from our house. I guessed there was some mischief contriving, when I observed my master and his friend whispering long together, sometimes pointing at me; and my fears made me fancy that I overheard and understood some of their words. But, the next morning Glumdalclitch my little nurse told me the whole matter, which she had cunningly picked out from her mother. The poor girl laid me on her bosom, and fell a weeping with shame and grief. She apprehended some mischief would happen to me from rude vulgar folks, who might squeeze me to death, or break one of my limbs by taking me in their hands. She had also observed how modest I was in my nature, how nicely I regarded my honour, and what an indignity I should conceive it to be exposed for money as a public spectacle to the meanest of the people. She said, her Papa and Mamma had promised that Grildrig should be hers, but now she found they meant to serve her as they did last year, when they pretended to give her a lamb, and yet, as soon as it was fat, sold it to a butcher. For my own part, I may truly affirm that I was less concerned than my nurse. I had a strong hope which never left me, that I should one day recover my liberty; and as to the ignominy of being carried about for a monster, I considered myself to be a perfect stranger in the country, and that such a misfortune could never be charged upon me as a reproach if ever I should return to England; since the king of Great Britain himself, in my condition, must have undergone the same distress.

My master, pursuant to the advice of his friend, carried me in a box the next market-day to the neighbouring town, and took along with him his little daughter my nurse upon a pillion behind him. The box was close on every side, with a little door for me to go in and out, and a few gimlet-holes to let in air. The girl had been so careful to put the quilt of her baby's bed into it, for me to lie down on. However, I was terribly shaken and discomposed in this journey, although it were but of half an hour. For the horse went about forty foot at every step, and trotted so high, that the agitation was equal to the rising and falling of a ship in a great storm, but much more frequent: our journey was somewhat further than from London to St Albans. My master

nicely: carefully
ignominy: shame
monster: freak
pillion: seat
gimlet-holes: small, narrow holes
agitation: movement

COMMENTARY
Glumdalclitch is worried for Gulliver's safety and is ashamed that they are going to treat him like a freak. Gulliver, however, is convinced that he will escape one day. He is carried in a box to market, the journey being extremely uncomfortable.

alighted at an inn which he used to frequent; and after consulting a while with the inn-keeper, and making some necessary preparations, he hired the *grultrud*, or crier, to give notice through the town, of a strange creature to be seen at the sign of the green eagle, not so big as a *splacknuck* (an animal in that country very finely shaped, about six foot long) and in every part of the body resembling an human creature, could speak several words, and perform an hundred diverting tricks.

I was placed upon a table in the largest room of the inn, which might be near three hundred foot square. My little nurse stood on a low stool close to the table, to take care of me, and direct what I should do. My master, to avoid a crowd, would suffer only thirty people at a time to see me. I walked about on the table as the girl commanded; she asked me questions as far as she knew my understanding of the language reached, and I answered them as loud as I could. I turned about several times to the company, paid my humble respects, said they were welcome, and used some other speeches I had been taught. I took up a thimble filled with liquor, which Glumdalclitch had given me for a cup, and drank their health. I drew out my hanger, and flourished with it after the manner of fencers in England. My nurse gave me part of a straw, which I exercised as a pike, having learned the art in my youth. I was that day shown

crier: person who announced news
exercised as a pike: used as a spear as in a military drill

to twelve sets of company, and as often forced to go over again with the same fopperies, till I was half dead with weariness and vexation. For those who had seen me made such wonderful reports, that the people were ready to break down the doors to come in. My master for his own interest would not suffer any one to touch me, except my nurse; and, to prevent danger, benches were set round the table at such a distance, as put me out of everybody's reach. However, an unlucky school-boy aimed a hazel nut directly at my head, which very narrowly missed me; otherwise, it came with so much violence, that it would have infallibly knocked out my brains; for it was almost as large as a small pumkin: but I had the satisfaction to see the young rogue well beaten, and turned out of the room.

My master gave public notice, that he would show me again the next market-day: and in the meantime, he prepared a more convenient vehicle for me, which he had reason enough to do; for I was so tired with my first journey, and with entertaining company eight hours together, that I could hardly stand upon my legs, or speak a word. It was at least three days before I recovered my strength; and that I might have no rest at home, all the neighbouring gentlemen from an hundred miles round, hearing of my fame, came to see me at my master's own house. There could not be fewer than thirty persons with their wives and children, (for the country is very populous); and my master demanded the rate of a full room whenever he showed me at home, although it were only to a single family. So that for some time I had but little ease every day of the week (except Wednesday, which is their sabbath) although I were not carried to the town.

My master, finding how profitable I was like to be, resolved to carry me to the most considerable cities of the kingdom. Having therefore provided himself with all things necessary for a long journey, and settled his affairs at home, he took leave of his wife, and upon the 17th of August 1703, about two months after my arrival, we set out for the metropolis, situated near the middle of that Empire, and about three thousand miles distance from our house: my master made his daughter Glumdalclitch ride behind him. She

COMMENTARY

Gulliver's performances are extremely popular and he becomes weary doing the same routines time after time. On one occasion a boy throws a nut at him, which would have killed him if it had been on target. Gulliver is put on show on every market day and also has to put on performances to people who visit the farmer's house. The farmer, seeing how profitable Gulliver's act is, decides to take Gulliver around the kingdom, putting on performances on the way.

fopperies: foolish acts
vexation: irritation
pumkin: pumpkin

carried me on her lap in a box tied about her waist. The girl had lined it on all sides with the softest cloth she could get, well quilted underneath, furnished it with her baby's bed, provided me with linen and other necessaries, and made everything as convenient as she could. We had no other company but a boy of the house, who rode after us with the luggage.

My master's design was to show me in all the towns by the way, and to step out of the road for fifty or an hundred miles, to any village or person of quality's house where he might expect custom. We made easy journies of not above seven or eight score miles a day: for Glumdalclitch, on purpose to spare me, complained she was tired with the trotting of the horse. She often took me out of my box at my own desire, to give me air, and show me the country, but always held me fast by leading strings. We passed over five or six rivers many degrees broader and deeper than the Nile or the Ganges; and there was hardly a rivulet so small as the Thames at London Bridge. We were ten weeks in our journey, and I was shown in eighteen large towns, besides many villages and private families.

On the 26th day of October, we arrived at the metropolis, called in their language *Lorbrulgrud*, or *Pride of the Universe*. My master took a lodging in the principal street of the city, not far from the royal palace, and put out bills in the usual form, containing an exact description of my person and parts. He hired a large room between three and four hundred foot wide. He provided a table sixty foot in diameter, upon which I was to act my part, and palisadoed it round three foot from the edge, and as many high, to prevent my falling over. I was shown ten times a day to the wonder and satisfaction of all people. I could now speak the language tolerably well, and perfectly understood every word that was spoken to me. Besides, I had learned their alphabet, and could make a shift to explain a sentence here and there; for Glumdalclitch had been my instructer while we were at home, and at leisure hours during our journey. She carried a little book in her pocket, not much larger than a Sanson's Atlas; it was a common treatise for the use of young girls, giving a short account of their religion; out of this she taught me my letters, and interpreted the words.

COMMENTARY

Gulliver is taken to the capital city, Lorbrulgrud, in his box, which Glumdalclitch has lined with cloth and filled with toy furniture so that his travels will be more comfortable. On the journey he comments on the large distances they travel and the huge rivers he sees. Glumdalclitch continues to teach him the language and his fluency steadily improves.

rivulet: small stream
bills: advertisements
parts: abilities
palisadoed: fenced
tolerably: reasonably
Sanson's Atlas: seventeenth-century atlas
treatise: serious book that discusses principles

3

Look out for . . .
- **Gulliver's change in fortunes once he is at court.**
- **the king's view of England.**
- **the rivalry between the queen's dwarf and Gulliver.**

The author sent for to court. The queen buys him of his master the farmer, and presents him to the king. He disputes with his majesty's great scholars. An apartment at court provided for the author. He is in high favour with the queen. He stands up for the honour of his own country. His quarrels with the queen's dwarf.

The frequent labours I underwent every day, made in a few weeks a very considerable change in my health: the more my master got by me, the more unsatiable he grew. I had quite lost my stomach, and was almost reduced to a skeleton. The farmer observed it, and concluding I soon must die, resolved to make as good a hand of me as he could. While he was thus reasoning and resolving with himself, a *slardal*, or gentleman usher, came from court, commanding my master to bring me immediately thither for the diversion of the queen and her ladies. Some of the latter had already been to see me, and reported strange things of my beauty, behaviour, and good sense. Her majesty and those who attended her, were beyond measure delighted with my demeanour. I fell on my knees, and begged the honour of kissing her imperial

disputes: argues
unsatiable: greedy
as good a hand: as much use
gentleman usher: an official from the court
demeanour: manner

COMMENTARY
Gulliver is so weary from all his performances he feels he is close to death. The queen sends for Gulliver and is delighted with him.

foot; but this gracious princess held out her little finger towards me (after I was set on a table) which I embraced in both my arms, and put the tip of it, with the utmost respect, to my lip. She made me some general questions about my country and my travels, which I answered as distinctly and in as few words as I could. She asked, whether I would be content to live at court. I bowed down to the board of the table, and humbly answered, that I was my master's slave, but if I were at my own disposal, I should be proud to devote my life to her majesty's service. She then asked my master whether he were willing to sell me at a good price. He, who apprehended I could not live a month, was ready enough to part with me, and demanded a thousand pieces of gold, which were ordered him on the spot, each piece being about the bigness of eight hundred moidores: but, allowing for the proportion of all things between that country and Europe, and the high price of gold among them, was hardly so great a sum as a thousand guineas would be in England. I then said to the queen, since I was now her majesty's most humble creature and vassal, I must beg the favour, that Glumdalclitch, who had always tended me with so much care and

COMMENTARY

The queen asks to buy Gulliver. The farmer is happy to sell him as he feels Gulliver will soon die anyway. Gulliver is pleased that he is now under the queen's protection but asks that Glumdalclitch be kept at court too.

moidores: gold coins
vassal: a subject who works as a servant in return for protection

kindness, and understood to do it so well, might be admitted into her service, and continue to be my nurse and instructor. Her majesty agreed to my petition, and easily got the farmer's consent, who was glad enough to have his daughter preferred at court: and the poor girl herself was not able to hide her joy. My last master withdrew, bidding me farewell, and saying he had left me in a good service; to which I replied not a word, only making him a slight bow.

The queen observed my coldness, and when the farmer was gone out of the apartment, asked me the reason. I made bold to tell her majesty that I owed no other obligation to my late master, than his not dashing out the brains of a poor harmless creature found by chance in his field; which obligation was amply recompensed by the gain he had made in showing me through half the kingdom, and the price he had now sold me for. That the life I had since led, was laborious enough to kill an animal of ten times my strength. That my health was much impaired by the continual drudgery of entertaining the rabble every hour of the day, and that if my master had not thought my life in danger, her majesty perhaps would not have got so cheap a bargain. But as I was out of all fear of being ill treated under the protection of so great and good an Empress, the ornament of nature, the darling of the world, the delight of her subjects, the phoenix of the creation; so, I hoped my late master's apprehensions would appear to be groundless; for I already found my spirits to revive by the influence of her most august presence.

This was the sum of my speech, delivered with great improprieties and hesitation; the latter part was altogether framed in the style peculiar to that people, whereof I learned some phrases from Glumdalclitch, while she was carrying me to court.

The queen giving great allowance for my defectiveness in speaking, was however surprised at so much wit and good sense in so diminutive an animal. She took me in her own hand, and carried me to the king, who was then retired to his cabinet. His majesty, a prince of much gravity, and austere countenance, not well observing my shape at first view, asked the queen after a cold manner, how long it was since she grew fond of a *splacknuck*; for such it

---

preferred at: promoted to
recompensed: repaid
drudgery: hard work
the phoenix of the creation: the most
   beautiful part of nature
august: dignified
great improprieties: many mistakes
defectiveness: imperfection
gravity: seriousness
austere: stern

COMMENTARY
Glumdalclitch is allowed to stay with Gulliver and she is tearful with joy. Gulliver then tells the queen why he was not fond of the farmer. The queen presents him to the king who at first mistakes him for an animal.

seems he took me to be, as I lay upon my breast in her majesty's right hand. But this princess, who hath an infinite deal of wit and humour, set me gently on my feet upon the scrutore; and commanded me to give his majesty an account of myself, which I did in a very few words; and Glumdalclitch, who attended at the cabinet door, and could not endure I should be out of her sight, being admitted, confirmed all that had passed from my arrival at her father's house.

FAST FORWARD: to page 111

The king, although he be as learned a person as any in his dominions and had been educated in the study of philosophy, and particularly mathematics; yet when he observed my shape exactly, and saw me walk erect, before I began to speak, conceived I might be a piece of clock-work (which is in that country arrived to a very great perfection), contrived by some ingenious artist. But, when he heard my voice, and found what I delivered to be regular and rational, he could not conceal his astonishment. He was by no means satisfied with the relation I gave him of the manner I came into his kingdom, but thought it a story concerted between Glumdalclitch and her father, who had taught me a set of words to make me sell at a higher price. Upon this imagination he put several other questions to me, and still received rational answers, no otherwise defective than by a foreign accent, and an imperfect knowledge in the language, with some rustic phrases which I had learned at the farmer's house, and did not suit the polite style of a court.

His majesty sent for three great scholars who were then in their weekly waiting (according to the custom in that country). These gentlemen, after they had a while examined my shape with much nicety, were of different opinions concerning me. They all agreed that I could not be produced according to the regular laws of nature, because I was not framed with a capacity of preserving

COMMENTARY
The king does not believe that Gulliver is a real human, thinking that he may be some clever clockwork toy. He calls in his advisers who puzzle over Gulliver.

scrutore: writing table
rustic: country
in their weekly waiting: on duty
nicety: care
was not framed with: did not have

my life, either by swiftness, or climbing of trees, or digging holes in the earth. They observed by my teeth, which they viewed with great exactness, that I was a carnivorous animal; yet most quadrupeds being an overmatch for me, and field mice, with some others, too nimble, they could not imagine how I should be able to support myself, unless I fed upon snails and other insects, which they offered by many learned arguments to evince that I could not possibly do. One of them seemed to think that I might be an embryo, or abortive birth. But this opinion was rejected by the other two, who observed my limbs to be perfect and finished; and that I had lived several years, as it was manifested from my beard, the stumps whereof they plainly discovered through a magnifying glass. They would not allow me to be a dwarf, because my littleness was beyond all degrees of comparison; for the queen's favourite dwarf, the smallest ever known in the kingdom, was near thirty foot high. After much debate, they concluded unanimously that I was only *relplum scalcath*, which is interpreted literally lusus naturae; a determination exactly agreeable to the modern philosophy of Europe: whose professors, disdaining the old evasion of occult causes, whereby the followers of Aristotle endeavour to vain to disguise their ignorance, have invented this wonderful solution of all difficulties, to the unspeakable advancement of human knowledge.

After this decisive conclusion, I entreated to be heard a word or two. I applied myself to the king, and assured his majesty, that I came from a country which abounded with several million of both sexes, and of my own stature; where the animals, trees, and houses were all in proportion; and where by consequence I might be able to defend myself, and to find sustenance, as any of his majesty's subjects could do here; which I took for a full answer to those gentlemens arguments. To this they only replied with a smile of contempt, saying that the farmer had instructed me very well in my lesson. The king, who had a much better understanding, dismissing his learned men, sent for the farmer, who by good fortune was not yet gone out of town: having therefore first examined him privately, and then confronted him with me and the young girl, his majesty began to think that what we told him might

---

evince: show
lusus naturae: a freak of nature, one of a
    kind
evasion of occult causes: excuse of
    supernatural causes
stature: size
sustenance: food

COMMENTARY
The king's advisers think that Gulliver is too defenseless and too small for a normal creature as he would be unable to kill for food to survive. One wonders whether Gulliver is an embryo but on closer inspection they see he has a beard. Eventually they decide that he is a one of a kind and seem to think that is a satisfactory explanation. Gulliver speaks up for himself and says that there are millions of others like him and that he is perfectly normal.

possibly be true. He desired the queen to order, that a particular care should be ◀◀
taken of me, and was of opinion, that Glumdalclitch should still continue in
her office of tending me, because he observed we had a great affection for each
other. A convenient apartment was provided for her at court; she had a sort of
governess appointed to take care of her education, a maid to dress her, and two
other servants for menial offices; but the care of me was wholly appropriated
to herself. The queen commanded her own cabinet-maker to contrive a box
that might serve me for a bed-chamber, after the model that Glumdalclitch
and I should agree upon. This man was a most ingenious artist, and according
to my directions, in three weeks finished for me a wooden chamber of sixteen
foot square, and twelve high; with sash windows, a door, and two closets, like a
London bed-chamber. The board that made the ceiling was to be lifted up and
down by two hinges, to put in a bed ready furnished by her majesty's
upholsterer, which Glumdalclitch took out every day to air, made it with her
own hands, and letting it down at night, locked up the roof over me. A nice
workman, who was famous for little curiosities, undertook to make me two
chairs, with backs and frames, of a substance not unlike ivory; and two tables,
with a cabinet to put my things in. The room was quilted on all sides, as well
as the floor and the ceiling, to prevent any accident from the carelessness of
those who carried me, and to break the force of a jolt when I went in a coach. I
desired a lock for my door to prevent rats and mice from coming in: the smith
after several attempts made the smallest that was ever seen among them; for I
have known a larger at the gate of a gentleman's house in England. I made a

---

REWIND: . . . possibly be true.
Gulliver is presented to the king who cannot believe that he is real but
instead thinks he may be a clockwork toy. When this is disproved, he
calls in three wise men who eventually decide that he must be a freak, a one of a
kind. Gulliver explains to the king that there are millions of others like him and after
the king checks Gulliver's story with the farmer he begins to believe him.

COMMENTARY
The king is still doubtful and sends for
the farmer. Having spoken to him, he
eventually begins to believe Gulliver's
story. He tells Glumdalclitch to
continue acting as nurse to Gulliver
and provides her with her own room.
A very elaborate wooden box is built
for Gulliver, which is fully furnished as a
gentleman's room.

shift to keep the key in a pocket of my own, fearing Glumdalclitch might lose it. The queen likewise ordered the thinnest silks that could be gotten, to make me clothes; not much thicker than an English blanket, very cumbersome till I was accustomed to them. They were after the fashion of the kingdom, partly resembling the Persian, and partly the Chinese; and are a very grave decent habit.

The queen became so fond of my company, that she could not dine without me. I had a table placed upon the same at which her majesty eat, just at her left elbow, and a chair to sit on. Glumdalclitch stood upon a stool on the floor, near my table, to assist and take care of me. I had an entire set of silver dishes and plates, and other necessaries, which in proportion to those of the queen, were not much bigger than what I have seen in a London toy-shop, for the furniture of a baby-house: these my little nurse kept in her pocket, in a silver box, and gave me at meals as I wanted them, always cleaning them herself. No person dined with the queen but the two princesses royal, the elder sixteen years old, and the younger at that time thirteen and a month. Her majesty used to put a bit of meat upon one of my dishes, out of which I carved for

necessaries: essentials

COMMENTARY
Gulliver is provided with some new clothes, which are specially made for him. Though made of the finest thread in the country, they still feel as thick as blankets to Gulliver. He is so popular with the queen that he eats with her and the two princesses every day. A special set of cutlery is made for him.

myself; and her diversion was to see me eat in miniature. For the queen (who had indeed but a weak stomach) took up at one mouthful, as much as a dozen English farmers could eat at a meal, which to me was for some time a very nauseous sight. She would craunch the wing of a lark, bones and all, between her teeth, although it were nine times as large as that of a full grown turkey; and put a bit of bread in her mouth, as big as two twelve-penny loaves. She drank out of a golden cup, above a hogshead at a draught. Her knives were twice as long as a scythe set straight upon the handle. The spoons, forks, and other instruments were all in the same proportion. I remember when Glumdalclitch carried me out of curiosity to see some of the tables at court, where ten or a dozen of these enormous knives and forks were lifted up together; I thought I had never till then beheld so terrible a sight.

It is the custom, that every Wednesday (which as I have before observed, was their sabbath), the king and queen, with the royal issue of both sexes, dine together in the apartments of his majesty, to whom I was now become a favourite; and at these times my little chair and table were placed at his left hand before one of the salt-cellers. This prince took a pleasure in conversing with me, enquiring into the manners, religion, laws, government, and learning of Europe, wherein I gave him the best account I was able. His apprehension was so clear, and his judgment so exact, that he made very wise reflexions and observations upon all I said. But, I confess, that after I had been a little too copious in talking of my own beloved country; of our trade, and wars by sea and lane, of our schisms in religion, and parties in the state; the prejudices of his education prevailed so far, that he could not forbear taking me up in his right hand, and stroking me gently with the other; after an hearty fit of laughing, asked me whether I were a Whig or a Tory. Then turning to his first minister, who waited behind him with a white staff, near as tall as the main-mast of the *Royal Sovereign*; he observed, how contemptible a thing was human grandeur, which could be mimicked by such diminutive insects as I; and yet, said he, I dare engage, those creatures have their titles and distinctions of honour; they contrive little nests and burrows, that they call houses and cities;

COMMENTARY
Gulliver describes the vast quantity of food the queen eats, although by the standards of her country she eats very little. Every Wednesday, which is like a Sunday in England, Gulliver eats with the king and queen together. On these occasions the king likes to ask him about life in England. After his discussions with Gulliver, the king often laughs at how people so small can still think of themselves so highly by giving themselves titles and building cities.

craunch: crunch
apprehension: understanding
copious: wordy
schisms: splits

Whig or a Tory: the two main political parties in England at the time
contemptible: laughable

they make a figure in dress and equipage; they love, they fight, they dispute, they cheat, they betray. And thus he continued on, while my colour came and went several times, with indignation to hear our noble country, the mistress of arts and arms, the scourge of France, the arbitress of Europe, the seat of virtue, piety, honour, and truth, the price and envy of the world, so contemptuously treated.

But, as I was not in a condition to resent injuries, so, upon mature thoughts, I began to doubt whether I were injured or no. For, after having been accustomed several months to the sight and converse of this people, and observed every object upon which I cast mine eyes, to be of proportionable magnitude, the horror I had first conceived from their bulk and aspect was so far worn off, that if I had then beheld a company of English lords and ladies in their finery and birthday clothes, acting their several parts in the most courtly manner of strutting, and bowing and prating; to say the truth, I should have been strongly tempted to laugh as much at them as this king and his grandees did at me. Neither indeed could I forbear smiling at myself, when the queen used to place me upon her hand towards a looking-glass, by which both our persons appeared before me in full view together; and there could nothing be more ridiculous than the comparison: so that I really began to imagine myself dwindled many degrees below my usual size.

Nothing angered and mortified me so much as the queen's dwarf, who being of the lowest stature that was ever in that country (for I verily think he was not full thirty foot high) became so insolent at seeing a creature so much beneath him, that he would always affect to swagger and look big as he passed by me in the queen's antichamber, while I was standing on some table talking with the lords or ladies of the court, and he seldom failed of a smart word or two upon my littleness; against which I could only revenge myself by calling him *brother*, challenging him to wrestle; and such repartees as are usual in the mouths of *court pages*. One day at dinner, this malicious little cub was so nettled with something I had said to him, that raising himself upon the frame of her majesty's chair, he took me up by the middle, as I was sitting down, not

equipage: horse-drawn carriage
arbitress: person who settles disputes
   between two parties, in this case two
   countries
magnitude: size
birthday clothes: fine clothes worn on the
   king's birthday
prating: speaking
grandees: nobles
dwindled: shrunk
mortified: humiliated
verily: truly
repartees: witty remarks

COMMENTARY
At first Gulliver feels very defensive about England, but after a while he begins to see things from the giants' point of view and says that he too would now find English lords and ladies ridiculous. Gulliver describes the problems he has had with the queen's dwarf who is envious of Gulliver's size and popularity with the queen.

thinking any harm, and let me drop into a large silver bowl of cream, and then ran away as fast as he could. I fell over head and ears, and if I had not been a good swimmer, it might have gone very hard with me; for Glumdalclitch in that instant happened to be at the other end of the room, and the queen was in such a fright, that she wanted presence of mind to assist me. But my little nurse ran to my relief, and took me out, after I had swallowed above a quart of cream. I was put to bed; however I received no other damage than the loss of a suit of clothes, which was utterly spoiled. The dwarf was soundly whipped, and as a further punishment,

forced to drink up the bowl of cream, into which he had thrown me; neither was he ever restored to favour; for, soon after the queen bestowed him to a lady of high quality, so that I saw him no more, to my very great satisfaction; for I could not tell to what extremity such a malicious urchin might have carried his resentment.

He had before served me a scurvy trick, which set the queen a laughing, although at the same time she were heartily vexed, and would have immediately cashiered him if I had not been so generous as to intercede. Her majesty had taken a marrow-bone upon her plate, and after knocking out the marrow, placed the bone again in the dish erect as it stood before; the dwarf watching his opportunity, while Glumdalclitch was gone to the sideboard, mounted the stool that she stood on to take care of me at meals; took me up on both hands and squeezing my legs together, wedged them into the marrow-bone above my waist; where I stuck for some time, and made a very ridiculous figure. I believe it was near a minute before any one knew what was become of

COMMENTARY

On one occasion the dwarf drops Gulliver in a bowl of cream, hoping to drown him. Fortunately, Glumdalclitch rescues him. The dwarf is punished, and Gulliver informs us that soon afterward he was sold off to another lady. On another occasion the dwarf pushed Gulliver into a bone after the marrow had been taken out.

quart: two pints (0.95 liters)
bestowed: gave
scurvy: mean
cashiered: fired
intercede: plead on his behalf

me; for I thought it below me to cry out. But, as princes seldom get their meat hot, my legs were not scalded, only my stockings and breeches in a sad condition. The dwarf at my entreaty had no other punishment than a sound whipping.

I was frequently rallied by the queen upon account of my fearfulness, and she used to ask me whether the people of my country were as great cowards as myself. The occasion was this. The kingdom is much pestered with flies in summer, and these odious insects, each of them as big as a Dunstable lark, hardly gave me any rest while I sat at dinner, with their continual humming and buzzing about mine ears. They would sometimes alight upon my victuals,

and leave their loathsome excrement or spawn behind, which to me was very visible, although not to the natives of that country, whose large optics were not so acute as mine in viewing smaller objects. Sometimes they would fix upon my nose or forehead, where they stung me to the quick, smelling very offensively, and I could easily trace that viscous matter, which our naturalists tell us enable those creatures to walk with their feet upwards upon a ceiling. I

excrement: droppings
optics: eyes
viscous: sticky

COMMENTARY
Gulliver describes his disgust at watching flies as big as birds leave their slimy trails and droppings on food. The giants are too large to see such things.

had much ado to defend myself against these detestable animals, and could not forbear starting when they came on my face. It was the common practice of the dwarf to catch a number of these insects in his hand, as school-boys do among us, and let them out suddenly under my nose, on purpose to frighten me, and divert the queen. My remedy was to cut them in pieces with my knife as they flew in the air, wherein my dexterity was much admired.

I remember one morning when Glumdalclitch had set me in my box upon a window, as she usually did in fair days to give me air (for I durst not venture to let the box be hung on a nail out of the window, as we do with cages in England) after I had lifted up one of my sashes, and sat down at my table to eat a piece of sweet cake for my breakfast, above twenty wasps, allured by the smell, came flying into the room, humming louder than the drones of as many bagpipes. Some of them seized my cake, and carried it piecemeal away, others flew about my head and face, confounding me with the noise, and putting me in the utmost terror of their stings. However I had the courage to rise and draw my hanger, and attack them in the air. I dispatched four of them but the rest got away, and I presently shut my window. These insects were as large as partridges; I took out their stings, found them an inch and a half long, and as sharp as needles. I carefully preserved them all, and having since shown them with some other curiosities in several parts of Europe, upon my return to England I gave three of them to Gresham College, and kept the fourth for myself.

COMMENTARY

Gulliver describes how the dwarf often released some huge flies under Gulliver's nose to amuse the queen. Gulliver had to fight them off with his sword. On another day he had to fight off a number of giant wasps that attacked him. He explains that he removed the stings from four of the dead ones and preserved them to take home to England.

sashes: sash windows
piecemeal: bit by bit

4

Look out for . . .
- the reasons why Brobdingnag is cut off from the rest of the world.
- the description of the beggars, which is made revolting by the fact that Gulliver sees things in much more detail because of his size.

The country described. A proposal for correcting modern maps. The king's palace, and some account of the metropolis. The author's way of travelling. The chief temple described.

I now intend to give the reader a short description of this country, as far as I travelled in it, which was not above two thousand miles round Lorbrulgrud the metropolis. For, the queen, whom I always attended, never went further when she accompanied the king in his progresses, and there stayed till his majesty returned from viewing his frontiers. The whole extent of this prince's dominions reacheth about six thousand miles in length, and from three to five in breadth. From when I cannot but conclude, that our geographers of Europe are in great error, by supposing nothing but sea between Japan and California; for it was ever my opinion, that there must be a balance of earth to counterpoise the great continent of Tartary; and therefore they ought to correct their maps and charts, by joining this vast tract of land to the north-west parts of America, wherein I shall be ready to lend them my assistance.

progresses: travels around the country
counterpoise: counterbalance
tract: area

COMMENTARY
Gulliver describes the kingdom of Brobdingnag. (See the map in the Introduction.)

The kingdom is a <u>peninsula</u>, terminated to the north-east by a ridge of mountains thirty miles high which <u>are altogether impassable</u> by reason of the volcanoes upon the tops. Neither do the most learned know what sort of mortals inhabit beyond those mountains, or whether they be inhabited at all. On the three other sides it is bounded by the ocean. There is not one seaport in the whole kingdom, and those parts of the coasts into which the rivers issue, are so full of pointed rocks, and the sea generally so rough, that there is no venturing with the smallest of their boats, so that these people are wholly excluded from any commerce with the rest of the world. But the large rivers are full of vessels, and abound with excellent fish, for they seldom get any from the sea, because the sea-fish are of the same size with those in Europe, and consequently not worth catching; whereby it is <u>manifest</u>, that nature in the production of plants and animals of so extraordinary a bulk, is wholly confined to this continent, of which I leave the reasons to be determined by philosophers. However, now and then they take a whale that happens to be

dashed against the rocks, which the common people feed on heartily. These whales I have known so large that a man could hardly carry one upon his shoulders; and sometimes for curiosity they are brought in hampers to Lorbrulgrud: I saw one of them in a dish at the king's table, which passed for a rarity, but I did not observe he was fond of it; for I think indeed the bigness disgusted him, although I have seen one somewhat larger in Greenland.

The country is well inhabited, for it contains fifty-one cities, near an hundred walled towns, and a great

COMMENTARY
The people of the country have no dealings with anyone else as they are closed in by volcanoes on one side and surrounded by dangerous rocks on the other three sides. Occasionally they catch whales from the sea, which they can carry on their backs. Everything in the country, however, is as huge as the people.

peninsula: a piece of land attached to the mainland
are altogether impassable: cannot be traveled through
manifest: clear

number of villages. To satisfy my curious reader, it may be sufficient to describe Lorbrulgrud. This city stands upon almost two equal parts on each side the river that passes through. It contains above eighty thousand houses. It is in length three *glonglungs* (which make about fifty-four English miles) and two and a half in breadth, as I measured it myself in the royal map made by the king's order, which was laid on the ground on purpose for me, and extended an hundred feet; I paced the diameter and circumference several times barefoot, and computing by the scale, measured it pretty exactly.

The king's palace is no regular edifice, but an heap of buildings above seven miles round: the chief rooms are generally two hundred and forty foot high, and broad and long in proportion. A coach was allowed to Glumdalclitch and me, wherein her governess frequently took her out to see the town, or go among the shops; and I was always of the party, carried in my box; although the girl at my own desire would often take me out, and hold me in her hand, that I might more conveniently view the houses and the people as we passed along the streets. I reckoned our coach to be about a square of Westminster Hall, but not altogether so high; however, I cannot be very exact. One day the governess ordered our coachman to stop at several shops; where the beggars watching their opportunity, crowded to the sides of the coach, and gave me the most horrible spectacles that ever an European eye beheld. There was a woman with a cancer in her breast, swelled to a monstrous size, full of holes, in two or three of which I could have easily crept, and covered my whole body. There was a fellow with a wen in his neck, larger than five woolpacks, and another with a couple of wooden legs, each about twenty foot high. But, the most hateful sight of all was the lice crawling on their clothes. I could see distinctly the limbs of these vermin with my naked eye, much better than those of an European louse through a microscope; and their snouts with which they rooted like swine. They were the first I had ever beheld, and I should have been curious enough to dissect one of them, if I had proper instruments (which I unluckily left behind me in the ship) although indeed the sight was so nauseous, that it perfectly turned my stomach.

edifice: building
a square of: a square with its sides the
   length of
wen: unnatural blister
rooted: burrowed

COMMENTARY
The capital city, Lorbrulgrud, is described. Gulliver tells us its size and describes the palace and the coach he travels in. On one occasion the coach is waiting for the queen to return from a shop and is surrounded by beggars. Gulliver describes with disgust their diseases and the lice that crawl on them.

FAST FORWARD: to page 123

Beside the large box in which I was usually carried, the queen ordered a smaller one to be made for me, of about twelve foot square, and ten high, for the convenience of travelling, because the other was somewhat too large for Glumdalclitch's lap, and cumbersome in the coach; it was made by the same artist, whom I directed in the whole contrivance. This travelling closet was an exact square with a window in the middle of three of the squares, and each window was latticed with iron wire on the outside, to prevent accidents in long journeys. On the fourth side, which had no window, two strong staples were fixed, through which the person that carried me, when I had a mind to be on horseback, put in a leathern belt, and buckled it about his waist. This was always the office of some grave trusty servant in whom I could confide, whether I attend the king and queen in their progresses, or were disposed to see the gardens, or pay a visit to some great lady or minister of state in the court, when Glumdalclitch happened to be out of order: for I soon began to be known and esteemed among the greatest officers, I suppose more upon account of their majesty's favour, than any merit of my own. In journeys, when I was weary of the coach, a servant on horseback would buckle my box, and place it on a cushion before him; and there I had a full prospect of the country on three sides from my three windows. I had in this closet a field-bed and a hammock hung from the ceiling, two chairs and a table, neatly screwed to the floor, to prevent being tossed about by the agitation of the horse or the coach. And having been long used to sea-voyages, those motions, although sometimes very violent, did not much discompose me.

Whenever I had a mind to see the town, it was always in my travelling-closet, which Glumdalclitch held in her lap in a kind of open sedan, after the fashion of the country, borne by four men, and attended by two others in the queen's livery. The people who had often heard of me, were very curious to

---

COMMENTARY

A small traveling box is made for Gulliver, which is fitted with furniture nailed to the floor. It has windows on three sides so that he can see out as he travels.

contrivance: project
latticed: crisscrossed
esteemed: respected
discompose: unsettle
sedan: carriage
borne: carried
queen's livery: uniform worn by the
    queen's servants

crowd about the sedan, and the girl was complaisant enough to make the bearers stop, and to take me in her hand that I might be more conveniently seen.

I was very desirous to see the chief temple, and particularly the tower belonging to it, which is reckoned the highest in the kingdom. Accordingly one day my nurse carried me thither, but I may truly say I came back disappointed; for the height is not above three thousand foot, reckoning from the ground to the highest pinnacle top; which allowing for the difference between the size of those people, and us in Europe, is no great matter for admiration, nor at all equal in proportion (if I rightly remember) to Salisbury steeple. But, not to detract from a nation to which during my life I shall acknowledge myself extremely obliged, it must be allowed that whatever this famous tower wants in height, is amply made up in beauty and strength. For the walls are near an hundred foot thick, built of hewn stone, whereof each is about forty foot square, and adorned on all sides with statues of gods and Emperors cut in marble larger than life, placed in their several niches. I measured a little finger which had fallen down from one of the statues, and lay unperceived among some rubbish, and found it exactly four foot and an inch in length. Glumdalclitch wrapped it up in a handkerchief, and carried it home in her pocket to keep among other trinkets, of which the girl was very fond, as children at her age usually are.

The king's kitchen is indeed a noble building, vaulted at top, and about six hundred foot high. The great oven is not so wide by ten paces as the cupola at St Paul's: for I measured the latter on purpose after my return. But if I should describe the kitchen-grate, the prodigious pots and kettles, the joints of meat turning on the spits, with many other particulars, perhaps I should be hardly believed; at least a severe critic would be apt to think I enlarged a little, as travellers are often suspected to do. To avoid which censure, I fear I have run too much into the other extreme; and that if this treatise should happen to be translated into the language of Brobdingnag (which is the general name of that kingdom), and transmitted thither, the king and his people would have

---

complaisant: obliging
pinnacle: steeple
Salisbury steeple: the tallest spire in England
detract: take away
hewn: cut
niches: spaces cut out in the wall
vaulted: arched
cupola: dome
censure: criticism
transmitted thither: carried there

COMMENTARY
Gulliver's coach is often stopped on journeys so that people can see him close-up. He describes the chief temple of the kingdom, which, though small considering the size of the people, is beautifully made. Gulliver describes with amazement the king's kitchen. He reassures his readers that he is not exaggerating and has, if anything, been too cautious in his descriptions.

reason to complain that I had done them an injury by a false and diminutive representation.

His majesty seldom keeps above six hundred horses in his stables: they are generally from fifty-four to sixty foot high. But, when he goes abroad on solemn days, he is attended for state by a militia guard of five hundred horse, which indeed I thought was the most splendid sight that could be ever beheld, til I saw part of his army in battalia, whereof I shall find another occasion to speak.

REWIND: . . . occasion to speak.
Gulliver describes a traveling box that is made for him to sit in, which is strapped to a servant's waist. He also describes some of the sights he sees while being carried around, including the temple, the king's kitchen, and the king's horses, all of which fill him with amazement.

COMMENTARY
Gulliver is impressed by the sight of the king's five hundred horses as they accompany him on visits around the kingdom.

diminutive representation: understated picture
battalia: battle order

Look out for . . .
- **the many incidents in this chapter that are a result of Gulliver's size. What do the Brobdingnagians think of him?**
- **the comments Gulliver makes about the foolishness of pretending to be something you are not.**

Several adventures that happened to the author. The execution of a criminal. The author shows his skill in navigation.

I should have lived happy enough in that country, if my littleness had not exposed me to several ridiculous and troublesome accidents; some of which I shall venture to relate. Glumdalclitch often carried me into the gardens of the court in my smaller box, and would sometimes take me out of it and hold me in her hand, or set me down to walk. I remember, before the dwarf left the queen, he followed us one day into those gardens; and my nurse having set me down, he and I being close together, near some dwarf apple-trees, I must need show my wit by a silly allusion between him and the trees, which happens to hold in their language as it doth in ours. Whereupon, the malicious rogue watching his opportunity, when I was walking under one of them, shook it directly over my head, by which a dozen apples, each of them near as large as a bristol barrel, came tumbling about my ears; one of them hit me on the back as I chanced to stoop, and knocked me down flat on my face, but I received no

allusion: connection
bristol barrel: barrels varied in size in different parts of the country

COMMENTARY
Gulliver describes a series of dangerous incidents that happened because of his size. Once, the dwarf shook an apple tree while Gulliver was under it and Gulliver was hit by a number of apples as big as barrels.

other hurt, and the dwarf was pardoned at my desire, because I have given the provocation.

Another day, Glumdalclitch left me on a smooth grass-plot to divert myself while she walked at some distance with her governess. In the meantime, there suddenly fell such a violent shower of hail, that I was immediately by the force of it struck to the ground: and when I was down, the hailstones gave me such cruel bangs all over the body, as if I had been pelted with tennis-balls; however

I made a shift to creep on all four, and shelter myself by lying flat on my face on the lee-side of a border of lemon thyme, but so bruised from head to foot, that I could not go abroad in ten days. Neither is this at all be wondered at, because nature in that country observing the same proportion through all her operations, a hailstone is near eighteen hundred times as large as one in Europe, which I can assert upon experience, having been so curious to weigh and measure them.

But, a more dangerous accident happened to me in the same garden, when my little nurse, believing she had put me in a secure place, which I often entreated her to do, that I might enjoy my own thoughts, and having left my

given the provocation: started the quarrel
operations: activities

box at home to avoid the trouble of carrying it, went to another part of the garden with her governess and some ladies of her acquaintance. While she was absent and out of hearing, a small white spaniel belonging to one of the chief gardeners, having got by accident into the garden, happened to range near the place where I lay. The dog following the scent, came directly up, and taking me in his mouth, ran straight to his master, wagging his tail, and set me gently on the ground. By good fortune he had been so well taught, that I was carried between his teeth without the least hurt, or even tearing my clothes. But, the poor gardener, who knew me well, and had a great kindness for me, was in a terrible fright. He gently took me up in both his hands, and asked me how I did; but I was so amazed and out of breath, that I could not speak a word. In a few minutes I came to myself, and he carried me safe to my little nurse, who by this time had returned to the place where she left me, and was in cruel agonies when I did not appear, nor answer when she called: she severely reprimanded the gardener on account of his dog. But, the thing was hushed up, and never known at court; for the girl was afraid of the queen's anger, and truly as to myself, I thought it would not be for my reputation that such a story should go about.

This accident absolutely determined Glumdalclitch never to trust me abroad for the future out of her sight. I had been long afraid of this resolution, and therefore concealed from her some little unlucky adventures that happened in those times when I was left by myself. Once a kite hovering over the garden, made a stoop at me, and if I had not resolutely drawn my hanger, and run under a thick espalier, he would have certainly carried me away in his

resolution: decision
stoop: swoop
espalier: ornamental shrub or fruit tree

COMMENTARY
Gulliver continues to describe dangerous events in his time in Brobdingnag. He is picked up by a spaniel and attacked by a bird of prey.

talons. Another time, walking to the top of a fresh mole-hill, I fell to my neck in the hole through which that animal had cast upon the earth, and coined some lie not worth remembering, to excuse myself for spoiling my clothes. I likewise broke my right shin against the shell of a snail, which I happened to stumble over, as I was walking alone, and thinking on poor England.

I cannot tell whether I was more pleased or mortified to observe in those solitary walks, that the smaller birds did not appear to be at all afraid of me; but would hop about within a yard distance, looking for worms and other food with as much indifference and security as if no creature at all were near them. I remember, a thrush had the confidence to snatch out of my hand with his bill, a piece of cake that Glumdalclitch had just given me for my breakfast. When I attempted to catch any of these birds, they would boldly turn against me, endeavouring to pick my fingers, which I durst not venture within their reach; and then they would hop back unconcerned to hunt for worms or snails, as they did before. But, one day I took a thick cudgel, and threw it with all my strength so luckily at a linnet, that I knocked him down, and seizing him by the neck with both my hands, ran with him in triumph to my nurse. However, the bird who had only been stunned, recovering himself, gave me so many boxes with his wings on both sides of my head and body, although I held him

COMMENTARY
Gulliver describes how he fell down a molehill, broke his shin on a snail, and captured a bird the size of a swan (which he later ate after a servant had broken its neck).

coined: made up
cudgel: large stick
boxes: blows

at arm's length, and was out of the reach of his claws, that I was twenty times thinking to let him go. But I was soon relieved by one of our servants, who wrung off the bird's neck; and I had him next day for dinner by the queen's command. This linnet, as near as I can remember, seemed to be somewhat larger than an English swan.

The maids of honour often invited Glumdalclitch to their apartments, and desired she would bring me along with her, on purpose to have the pleasure of seeing and touching me. They would often strip me naked from top to toe, and lay me at full length in their bosoms; wherewith I was much disgusted; because, to say the truth a very offensive smell came from their skins; which I do not mention or intend to the disadvantage of those excellent ladies, for whom I have all manner of respect: but, I conceive, that my sense was more acute in proportion to my littleness; and that those illustrious persons were no more disagreeable to their lovers, or to each other, than people of the same quality are with us in England. And, after all, I found their natural smell was much more supportable than when they used perfumes, under which I immediately swooned away. I cannot forget, that an intimate friend of mine in Lilliput took the freedom in a warm day, when I had used a good deal of exercise, to complain of a strong smell about me; although I am as little faulty that way as most of my sex: but I suppose, his faculty of smelling was as nice with regard to me, as mine was to that of this people. Upon this point, I cannot forbear doing justice to the queen my mistress, and Glumdalclitch my nurse, whose persons were as sweet as those of any lady in England.

That which gave me most uneasiness among these maids of honour, when my nurse carried me to visit them, was to see them use me without any manner of ceremony, like a creature who had no sort of consequence. For, they would strip themselves to the skin, and put on their smocks in my presence, while I was placed on their toilet directly before their naked bodies, which, I am sure, to me was very far from being a tempting sight, or from giving me any other motions than those of horror and disgust. Their skins appeared so coarse and uneven, so variously colored when I saw them near, with a mole

COMMENTARY
Gulliver explains that he was seen as a plaything by the queen's attendants. He says that he found their smell unpleasant when he was close to them but realizes that this is again to do with their size as he was smelly to the Lilliputians. He concludes that they probably smelled fine to each other. He is embarrassed by the lack of modesty the women show in his presence as they see him more as a toy than a man. He says that he does not find them attractive when they undress as their skin appears to him to be discolored and hairy.

maids of honour: queen's attendants   *manner of ceremony*: formality
swooned away: fainted   *consequence*: importance
nice: precise   *toilet*: dressing table

here and there as broad as a trencher, and hairs hanging from it thicker than pack-threads; to say nothing further concerning the rest of their persons. Neither did they at all scruple while I was by, to discharge what they had drunk, to the quantity of at least two hogsheads, in a vessel that held above three tuns. The handsomest among these maids of honour, a pleasant frolicsome girl of sixteen, would sometimes set me astride upon one of her nipples, with many other tricks, wherein the reader will excuse me for not being over particular. But, I was so much displeased, that I entreated Glumdalclitch to contrive some excuse for not seeing that young lady any more.

One day, a young gentleman who was nephew to my nurse's governess, came and pressed them both to see an execution. It was of a man who had murdered one of that gentleman's intimate acquaintance. Glumdalclitch was prevailed on to be of the company, very much against her inclination, for she

was naturally tender hearted: and, as for myself, although I abhorred such kind of spectacles; yet my curiosity tempted me to see something that I thought must be extraordinary. The malefactor was fixed in a chair upon a scaffold erected for the purpose; and his head cut off at one blow with a sword of about forty foot long. The veins and arteries spouted up such a prodigious quantity of blood, and so high in the air, that the great *jet d'eau* at Versailles was not equal for the time it lasted; and the head when it fell on the scaffold floor, gave such a bounce, as made me start, although I were at least an English mile distant.

COMMENTARY

Gulliver explains that he tried to find excuses to avoid meeting one of the young women who treated him in a particularly embarrassing way. Glumdalclitch and Gulliver observe an execution, which he describes in gory detail.

trencher: a wooden serving tray
hogsheads: one hogshead is 63 gallons (238 l.)
three tuns: 756 gallons (2,858 l.)
frolicsome: playful
over particular: too explicit
contrive: invent
inclination: wish
abhorred: despised
malefactor: criminal
jet d'eau: fountain

FAST FORWARD: to page 131

The queen, who often used to hear me talk of my sea-voyages, and took all occasions to divert me when I was melancholy, asked me whether I understood how to handle a sail or an oar, and whether a little exercise of rowing might not be convenient for my health. I answered, that I understood both very well. For although my proper employment had been to be surgeon or doctor to the ship, yet often upon a pinch, I was forced to work like a common mariner. But, I could not see how this could be done in their country, where the smallest wherry was equal to a first rate man of war among us: and such a boat as I could manage, would never live in any of their rivers: her majesty said, if I would contrive a boat, her own joiner should make it, and she would provide a place for me to sail in. The fellow was an ingenious workman, and by my instructions in ten days finished a pleasure-boat with all its tackling, able conveniently to hold eight Europeans. When it was finished, the queen was so delighted, that she ran with it in her lap to the king, who ordered it to be put in a cistern full of water, with me in it, by way of trial; where I could not manage my two sculls or little oars for want of room. But, the queen had before contrived another project. She ordered the joiner to make a wooden trough of three hundred foot long, fifty broad, and eight deep; which being well pitched to prevent leaking, was placed on the floor along the wall, in an outer room of the palace. It had a cock near the bottom, to let out the water when it began to grow stale, and two servants could easily fill it in half an hour. Here I often used to row for my diversion, as well as that of the queen and her ladies, who thought themselves agreeably entertained with my skill and agility. Sometimes I would put up my sail, and then my business was only to steer, while the ladies gave me a gale with their fans; and when they were weary, some of the pages would blow my sail forward with their breath, while I showed my art by steering starboard or larboard as I pleased. When I had

convenient: good
upon a pinch: if needed
wherry: rowboat
joiner: carpenter
tackling: the ropes on a boat for controling sails, etc.
cistern: water tank
sculls: oars
pitched: sealed with pitch
cock: plug
starboard or larboard: right or left

COMMENTARY
The queen wishes to see Gulliver demonstrate his sailing and rowing skills. A boat is built for him along with a wooden trough to sail in. The ladies of the court often move him along with their fans while at other times he is blown along by the servants.

done, Glumdalclitch always carried my boat into her closet, and hung it on a nail to dry.

In this exercise I once met an accident which had like to have cost me my life. For, one of the pages having put my boat into the trough, the governess who attended Glumdalclitch very officiously lifted me up to place me in the boat, but I happened to slip through her fingers, and should have infallibly fallen down forty foot upon the floor, if the luckiest chance in the world, I had not been stopped by a corking-pin that stuck in the good gentlewoman's stomacher; the head of the pin passed between my shirt and the waistband of my breeches; and thus I was held by the middle in the air, till Glumdalclitch ran to my relief.

Another time, one of the servants, whose office it was to fill my trough every third day with fresh water, was so careless to let a huge frog (not perceiving it) slip out of his pail. The frog lay concealed till I was put into my boat, but then seeing a resting place, climbed up, and made it lean so much on one side, that I was forced to balance it with all my weight on the other, to prevent overturning. When the frog was got in, it hopped at once half the length of the boat, and then over my head, backwards and forwards, daubing my face and clothes with its odious slime. The largeness of its features made it appear the most deformed animal that can be conceived. However, I desired Glumdalclitch to let me deal with it alone. I banged it a good while with one of my sculls, and at last forced it to leap out of the boat.

But the greatest danger I ever underwent in that kingdom, was from a monkey, who belonged to one of the clerks of the kitchen. Glumdalclitch had

---

REWIND: . . .out of the boat.

The queen, wishing to see Gulliver's rowing skills, has a boat built for him in which he rows in a trough. Sometimes he is blown along by the ladies' fans and sometimes by the servants' breath. On one occasion a giant frog gets into the trough and Gulliver has to beat it off with his oars.

COMMENTARY

Gulliver describes two accidents that happen while he is involved in his sailing demonstrations. On one occasion he is nearly dropped to the floor and is only saved by his clothes catching on a pin in one of the ladies' dresses. Another time he is almost sunk when a giant frog gets into his boat. He eventually beats it off with his oar.

officiously: proudly
corking-pin: very large pin
stomacher: patterned material worn on
 the stomach

locked me up in her closet, while she went somewhere upon business, or a visit. The weather being very warm, the closet window was left open, as well as the windows and the door of my bigger box, in which I usually lived, because of its largeness and conveniency. As I sat quietly *meditating* at my table, I heard something bounce in at the closet window, and skip about from one side to the other; whereat, although I were much alarmed, yet I ventured to look out, but not stirring from my seat; and then I saw this frolicsome animal, frisking and leaping up and down, till at last he came to my box, which he seemed to view with great pleasure and curiosity, peeping in at the door and every window. I retreated to the farther corner of my room, or box; but the monkey looking in at every side, put me into such a fright, that I *wanted presence of mind* to conceal myself under the bed, as I might easily have done. After some time spent in peeping, grinning, and chattering, he at last espied me; and reaching one of his paws in at the door, as a cat does when she plays with a mouse, although I often shifted place to avoid him; he at length seized the lappet of my coat (which being made of that country silk, was very thick and strong) and dragged me out. He took me up in his right forefoot, and held

meditating: thinking
wanted presence of mind: did not think

COMMENTARY
One day a giant monkey, belonging to one of the kitchen servants, steals Gulliver from his box.

me as a nurse doth a child she is going to suckle; just I have seen the same sort of creature do with a kitten in Europe: and when I offered to struggle, he squeezed me so hard, that I thought it more prudent to submit. I have good reason to believe that he took me for a young one of his own species, by his often stroking my face very gently with his other paw. In these diversions he was interrupted by a noise at the closet door, as if some body were opening it; whereupon he suddenly leaped up to the window at which he had come in, and thence upon the leads and gutters, walking upon three legs, and holding me in the fourth, till he clambered up to a roof that was next to ours. I heard Glumdalclitch give a shriek at the moment he was carrying me out. The poor girl was almost distracted: that quarter of the palace was all in an uproar; the servants ran for ladders; the monkey was seen by hundreds in the court, sitting upon the ridge of a building, holding me like a baby in one of his fore-paws, and feeding me with the other, by cramming into my mouth some victuals he had squeezed out of the bag on one side of his chaps, and patting me when I would not eat; whereat many of the rabble below could not forbear laughing; neither do I think they justly ought to be blamed; for without question, the sight was ridiculous enough to everybody but myself. Some of the people threw up stones, hoping to drive the monkey down; but this was strictly forbidden, or else very probably my brains had been dashed out.

The ladders were now applied, and mounted by several men; which the monkey observing, and finding himself almost encompassed; not being able to make speed enough with his three legs, let me drop on a ridge-tile, and made his escape. Here I sat for some time five hundred yards from the ground, expecting every moment to be blown down by the wind, or to fall by my own giddiness, and come tumbling over and over from the ridge to the eaves. But an honest lad, one of my nurse's footmen, climbed up, and putting me into his breeches pocket, brought me down safe.

I was almost choked with the filthy stuff the monkey had crammed down my throat; but, my dear little nurse picked it out of my mouth with a small needle; and then I fell a vomiting, which gave me great relief. Yet I was so weak

COMMENTARY

The monkey treats Gulliver like a baby monkey. When it hears someone come into the room it escapes onto the roof with Gulliver. The people of the palace try to rescue Gulliver. At first they throw stones at the monkey but stop this when they realize one may hit and kill Gulliver. Meanwhile, the monkey forcefeeds Gulliver with food it has stored up in its mouth. Eventually some people arrive on the roof and surround the monkey, which drops Gulliver and runs off. He is saved by a servant and taken into the palace where he is sick because of the food forced into him.

leads: lead used as roof covering
distracted: hysterical
chaps: cheeks

and bruised in the sides with the squeezes given me by this odious animal, that I was forced to keep my bed a fortnight. The king, queen, and all the court, sent every day to enquire after my health; and her majesty made me several visits during my sickness. The monkey was killed, and an order made that no such animal should be kept about the palace.

When I attended the king after my recovery, to return him thanks for his favours, he was pleased to rally me a good deal upon this adventure. He asked me what my thoughts and speculations were while I lay in the monkey's paw; how I liked the victuals he gave me, his manner of feeding; and whether the fresh air on the roof had sharpened my stomach. He desired to know what I would have done upon such an occasion in my own country. I told his majesty, that in Europe we had no monkeys, except such as were brought for curiosities from other places, and so small, that I could deal with a dozen of them together, if they presumed to attack me. And as for that monstrous animal with whom I was so lately engaged (it was indeed as large as an elephant), if my fears had suffered me to think so far as to make use of my hanger (looking fiercely, and clapping my hand upon the hilt as I spoke) when he poked his paw into my chamber, perhaps I should have given him such a wound, as would have made him glad to withdraw it with more haste than he put it in. This I delivered in a firm tone, like a person who was jealous lest his courage should be called in question. However, my speech produced nothing else besides a loud laughter; which all the respect due to his majesty from those about him, could not make them contain. This made me reflect, how vain at attempt it is for a man to endeavour doing himself honour among those who are out of all degree of equality or comparison with him. And yet I have seen the moral of my own behavior very frequent in England since my return; where a little contemptible varlet, without the least title to birth, person, wit, or common sense, shall presume to look importance, and put himself upon a foot with the greatest persons of the kingdom.

I was every day furnishing the court with some ridiculous story; and Glumdalclitch, although she loved me to excess, yet was arch enough to inform

rally: tease
speculations: opinions
sharpened my stomach: made me hungry
the moral: an example
varlet: rascal
put himself upon a foot with: feel equal to

COMMENTARY
The monkey is put down. The court finds Gulliver's adventure with the monkey funny and, at first, he is angry and tells them how brave he would have been in his own country. However, he begins to see that really he does appear to be a ridiculous figure in comparison to them. This makes him think of young men in England who, though quite pathetic, pretend to be something greater than they are.

the queen, whenever I committed any folly that she thought would be diverting to her majesty. The girl who had been out of order, was carried by her governess to take the air about an hour's distance, or thirty miles from town. They alighted out of the coach near a small footpath in a field; and Glumdalclitch setting down my travelling box, I went out of it to walk. There was a cow-dung in the path, and I must needs try my activity by attempting to leap over it. I took a run, but unfortunately jumped short, and found myself just in the middle up to my knees. I waded through with some difficulty, and one of the footmen wiped me as clean as he could with his handkerchief; for I was filthily bemired, and my nurse confined me to my box until we returned home; where the queen was soon informed of what had passed, and the footmen spread it about the court; so that all the mirth, for some days, was at my expense.

bemired: dirtied

COMMENTARY
Gulliver often provides laughter for the court, much to his embarrassment. On one occasion he is walking through a field and decides to jump over a giant cow pat. Unfortunately he lands right in it.

6

Look out for . . .
● **Gulliver's ability to invent things.**
● **Gulliver's detailed description of England and the king's response. Who do you think has the most accurate view of the country?**

Several contrivances of the author to please the king and queen. He shows his skill in music. The king enquires into the state of Europe, which the author relates to him. The king's observations thereon.

I used to attend the king's levee once or twice a week, and had often seen him under the barber's hand, which indeed was at first very terrible to behold. For, the razor was almost twice as long as an ordinary scythe. His majesty, according to the custom of the country, was only shaved twice a week. I once prevailed on the barber to give me some of the suds of the lather, out of which I picked forty or fifty of the strongest stumps of hair. I then took a piece of fine wood, and cut it like the back of a comb, making several holes in it at equal distance, with as small a needle as I could get from Glumdalclitch. I fixed in the stumps so artificially, scraping and sloping them with my knife towards the points, that I made a very tolerable comb; which was a seasonable supply, my own being so much broken in the teeth, that it was almost useless; neither did I know any artist in that country so nice and exact, as would undertake to make me another.

levee: a morning meeting held by a king just after getting up
prevailed on: persuaded
artificially: artfully

COMMENTARY
Gulliver displays his cleverness by making a comb using the bristles from the king's beard.

And this puts me in mind of an amusement wherein I spent many of my leisure hours. I desired the queen's woman to save for me the combings of her majesty's hair, whereof in time I got a good quantity; and consulting with my friend the cabinet-maker, who had received general orders to do little jobs for me; I directed him to make two chair frames, no larger than those I had in my box, and then to bore little holes with a fine awl round those parts where I designed the backs and seats; through these holes I wove the strongest hairs I could pick out, just after the manner of cane-chairs in England. When they were finished, I made a present of them to her majesty, who kept them in her

cabinet, and used to show them for curiosities; as indeed they were the wonder of everyone who beheld them. The queen would have had me sit upon one of these chairs, but I absolutely refused to obey her; protesting I would rather die a thousand deaths than place a dishonourable part of my body on those precious hairs that once adorned her majesty's head. Of these hairs (as I had always a mechanical genius) I likewise made a neat little purse about five foot long, with her majesty's name deciphered in gold letters, which I gave to

COMMENTARY
Gulliver builds some chairs for the queen using wood and strands of her hair. He also uses the queen's hair to make a purse for Glumdalclitch.

awl: tool for piercing wood
mechanical genius: skill in making things
deciphered: written

Glumdalclitch, by the queen's consent. To say the truth, it was more for show that use, being not of strength to bear the weight of some of the larger coins; and therefore she kept nothing in it, but some little toys that girls are fond of.

The king, who delighted in music, had frequent consorts at court, to which I was sometimes carried, and set in my box on a table to hear them: but, the noise was so great, that I could hardly distinguish the tunes. I am confident, that all the drums and trumpets of a royal army, beating and sounding together just at your ears, could not equal it. My practice was to have my box removed the places where the performers sat, as far as I could; then to shut the doors and windows of it, and draw the window-curtains; after which I found their music not disagreeable.

I had learned in my youth to play a little upon the spinet; Glumdalclitch kept one in her chamber, and a master attended twice a week to teach her: I call it a spinet, because it somewhat resembled that instrument, and was played upon in the same manner. A fancy came into my head, that I would entertain the king and queen with an English tune upon this instrument. But this appeared extremely difficult. For, the spinet was near sixty foot long, each key being almost a foot wide; so that, with my arms extended, I could not reach to above five keys; and to press them down required a good smart stroke with my fist, which would be too great a labour, and to no purpose. The method I contrived was this. I prepared two round sticks about the bigness of common cudgels; they were thicker at one end than the other, and I covered the thicker end with a piece of a mouse's skin, that by rapping on them, I might neither damage the tops of the keys, nor interrupt the sound. Before the spinet, a bench was placed about four feet below the keys, and I was put upon the bench. I ran sidelong upon it that way and this, as fast as I could, banging the proper keys with my two sticks; and made a shift to play a jig to the great satisfaction of both their majesties: but, it was the most violent exercise I ever underwent, and yet I could not strike above sixteen keys, nor, consequently, play the bass and treble together, as other artists do; which was a great disadvantage to my performance.

consorts: concerts
not disagreeable: quite pleasant
spinet: small, triangular-shaped keyboard
sideling: sideways

COMMENTARY
Gulliver liked to listen to the concerts performed at court. However, as they were so loud he had to sit in a different room in his box with the curtains closed in order to appreciate them. He also describes how he managed to play a spinet (a small harpsichord) by using two large sticks and running up and down a bench placed alongside the instrument.

FAST FORWARD: to page 152

The king, who as I before observed, was a prince of excellent understanding, would frequently order that I should be brought in my box, and set upon the table in his closet. He would then command me to bring one of my chairs out of the box, and sit down within three yards distance upon the top of the cabinet; which brought me almost to a level with his face. In this manner I had several conversations with him. I one day took the freedom to tell his majesty, that the contempt he discovered towards Europe, and the rest of the world, did not seem answerable to those excellent qualities of mind, that he was master of. That reason did not extend itself with the bulk of the body: on the contrary, we observed in our country, that the tallest persons were usually least provided with it. That among other animals, bees and ants had the reputation of more industry, art, and sagacity than many of the larger kinds. And that, as inconsiderable as he took me to be, I hoped I might live to do his majesty some signal service. The king heard me with attention; and began to conceive a much better opinion of me than he had ever before. He desired I would give him as exact an account of the government of England as I possibly could; because, as fond as princes commonly are of their own customs (for so he conjectured of other monarchs by my former discourses) he should be glad to hear of any thing that might deserve imitation.

Imagine with thyself, courteous reader, how often I then wished for the tongue of Demosthenes or Cicero, that might have enabled me to celebrate the praise of my own dear native country in a style equal to its merits and felicity.

I began my discourse by informing his majesty that our dominions consisted of two islands, which composed three mighty kingdoms under one sovereign, besides our plantations in America. I dwelt long upon the fertility of our soil, and the temperature of our climate. I then spoke at large upon the constitution of an English parliament, partly made up of an illustrious body

COMMENTARY

Gulliver often has conversations with the king about Europe. On one occasion Gulliver feels he has to explain to the king that just because his race is smaller it does not mean that they are less intelligent and that in their own country it is the larger people who are usually less intelligent. The king listens with respect and then asks Gulliver to give a full description of England. Gulliver wishes to do his best in singing its praises.

contempt he discovered: scorn he showed
That reason did not extend itself: that intelligence did not grow
industry: hard work
art: skill
sagacity: wisdom
signal: special
discourses: speeches
Demosthenes or Cicero: two great speakers from the past
plantations: colonies
illustrious: glorious

called the house of peers, persons of the noblest blood, and of the most ancient and ample patrimonies. I described that extraordinary care always taken of their education in arts and arms, to qualify them for being counsellors born to the king and kingdom, to have a share in the legislature, to be members of the highest court of judicature from whence there could be no appeal; and to be champions always ready for the defence of their prince and country by their valour, conduct and fidelity. That these were the ornament and bulwark of the kingdom, worthy followers of their most renowned ancestors, whose honour had been the reward of their virtue, from which their posterity were never once known to degenerate. To these were joined several holy persons, as part of that assembly, under the title of bishops; whose peculiar business it is, to take care of religion, and of those who instruct the people therein. These were searched and sought out through the whole nation, by the prince and wisest counsellors, among such of the priesthood, as were most deservedly distinguished by the sanctity of their lives, and the depth of their erudition; who were indeed the spiritual fathers of the clergy and the people.

That, the other part of the parliament consisted as an assembly called the house of commons; who were all principal gentlemen, *freely* picked and culled out by the people themselves, for their great abilities, and love of their country, to represent the wisdom of the whole nation. And, these two bodies make up the most august assembly in Europe, to whom, in conjunction with the prince, the whole legislature is committed.

I then descended to the courts of justice, over which the judges, those venerable sages and interpreters of the law, presided, for determining the disputed rights and properties of men, as well as for the punishment of vice, and protection of innocence. I mentioned the prudent management of our treasury; the valour and achievements of our forces by sea and land. I computed the number of our people, by reckoning how many millions there might be of each religious sect, or political party amongst us. I did not omit even our sports and pastimes, or any other particular which I thought might

COMMENTARY

Gulliver describes England's government, law, wars, leisure activities, and its history. He paints a glowing picture of a country in which people act honorably in everything they do. He says that Parliament is full of people who had either been born into great and honorable families (the Lords) or had been chosen to represent the people because of their wisdom or virtue. Swift is mocking Gulliver's naïve view of his country, which is so perfect it is obviously untrue. Swift is being ironic because he intends us to think the opposite of what Gulliver says.

patrimonies: inheritances	*bulwark*: defense	*culled out*: selected
legislature: Parliament	*degenerate*: worsen	*venerable*: worthy
judicature: lawyers	*erudition*: learning	

redound to the honour of my country. And, I finished all with a brief historical account of affairs and events in England for about an hundred years past.

This conversation was not ended under five audiences, each of several hours; and the king heard the whole with great attention; frequently taking notes of what I spoke, as well as memorandums of what questions he intended to ask me.

When I had put an end to these long discourses, his majesty in a sixth audience consulting his notes, proposed many doubts, queries, and objections, upon every article. He asked, what methods were used to cultivate the minds and bodies of our young nobility; and in what kind of business they commonly spent the first and teachable part of their lives. What course was taken to supply that assembly, when any noble family became extinct. What qualifications were necessary in those who are to be created new lords: whether the humour of the prince, a sum of money to a court lady, or a prime minister; or a design of strengthening a party opposite to the public interest, ever happened to be motives in those advancements. What share of knowledge these lords had in the laws of their country, and how they came by it, so as to enable them to decide the properties of their fellow-subjects in the last resort. Whether they were always so free from avarice, partialities, or want, that a bribe, or some other sinister view, could have no place among them. Whether those holy lords I spoke of, were constantly promoted to that rank upon account of their knowledge in religious matters, and the sanctity of their lives, had never been compliers with the times, while they were common priests; or slavish prostitute chaplains to some nobleman, whose opinions they continued servilely to follow after they were admitted into that assembly.

He then desired to know what arts were practised in electing those whom I called commoners. Whether, a stranger with a strong purse might not influence the vulgar voters to chose him before their own landlord, or the most considerable gentleman in the neighbourhood. How it came to pass, that people were so violently bent upon getting into this assembly, which I allowed to be a great trouble and expence, often to the ruin of their families, without

COMMENTARY

The king listens and takes notes. When Gulliver finishes the king questions him and raises doubts about this perfect country that Gulliver has described. He wonders if people become powerful through whom they know rather than ability and if they use their power to gain more money and influence.

advancements: promotions
properties: nature
partialities: bias
sinister view: treacherous idea
compliers with the times: people just fitting in with the latest fashion
slavish prostitute chaplains: priests who gain power through flattering a lord
servilely: slavishly
a strong purse: a lot of money
violently bent: utterly determined

redound: add advantage
opposite to the public interest: against the good of the country

any salary or pension: because this appeared such an exalted strain of virtue and public spirit, that his majesty seemed to doubt it might possibly not be always sincere: and he desired to know, whether such zealous gentlemen could have any views of refunding themselves for the charges and trouble they were at, by sacrificing the public good to the designs of a weak and vicious prince, in conjunction with a corrupted ministry. He multiplied his questions, and sifted me thoroughly upon every part of this head; proposing numberless enquiries and objections, which I think it not prudent or convenient to repeat.

Upon what I said in relation to our course of justice, his majesty desired to be satisfied in several points: and, this I was the better able to do, having been formerly almost ruined by a long suit in Chancery, which was decreed for me with costs. He asked, what time was usually spent in determining between right and wrong, and what degree of expence. Whether advocates and orators had liberty to plead in causes manifestly known to be unjust, vexatious, or oppressive. Whether party in religion or politics were observed to be of any weight in the scale of justice. Whether those pleading orators were persons educated in the general knowledge of equity, or only in provincial, national, and other local customs. Whether they or their judges had any part in penning those laws, which they assumed the liberty of interpreting and glossing upon at their pleasure. Whether they had ever at different times pleaded for and against the same cause, and cited precedents to prove contrary opinions. Whether they were a rich or a poor corporation. Whether they received any pecuniary reward for pleading or delivering their opinions. And particularly whether they were ever admitted as members in the lower senate.

He fell next upon the management of our treasury; and said, he thought my memory had failed me, because I computed our taxes at about five or six millions a year; and when I came to mention the issues, he found they sometimes amounted to more than double; for, the notes he had taken were very particular in this point; because he hoped, as he told me, that the knowledge of our conduct might be useful to him; and he could not be deceived in his calculations. But, if what I told him were true, he was still at a

COMMENTARY
The king wonders if lawyers are always fair or if they sometimes defend people to become wealthy. He suspects that lawyers will argue one thing one day and the opposite the next.

exalted strain of virtue: incredibly pure type of goodness	*vexatious*: without sufficient grounds for prosecution
in conjunction with: together with	*equity*: natural justice, fairness
head: subject	*glossing upon*: explaining
Chancery: a major law court	*cited precedents*: mentioned previous cases
advocates: lawyers	*pecuniary*: financial
manifestly: clearly	*lower senate*: House of Commons

loss how a kingdom could run out of its estate like a private person. He asked me, who were our creditors? and, where we found money to pay them? He wondered to hear me talk of such chargeable and extensive wars; that, certainly we must be a quarrelsome people, or live among very bad neighbours; and that our generals must needs be richer than our kings. He asked what business we had out of our own islands, unless upon the score of trade or treaty, or to defend the coasts with our fleet. Above all, he was amazed to hear me talk of a mercenary standing army in the midst of peace, and among a free people. He said, if we were governed by our own consent in the persons of our representatives, he could not imagine of whom we were afraid, or against whom we were to fight; and would hear my opinion, whether a private man's house might not better be defended by himself, his children, and family; than by half a dozen rascals picked up at a venture in the streets, for small wages, who might get an hundred times more by cutting their throats.

He laughed at my odd kind of arithmetic (as he was pleased to call it) in reckoning the numbers of our people by a computation drawn from the several sects among us in religion and politics. He said, he knew no reason, why those

COMMENTARY
The king does not understand how England can be in debt like a person. He goes on to say that English people must be very aggressive to be so often at war and to need an army even when there is no enemy.

estate: wealth
creditors: people owed money
chargeable: expensive
mercenary standing army: professional army in peace time
representatives: Members of Parliament

who entertain opinions prejudicial to the public, should be obliged to change, or should not be obliged to conceal them. And, as it was tyranny in any government to require the first, so it was weakness not to enforce the second: for, a man may be allowed to keep poisons in his closet, but not to vend them about as cordials.

He observed, that among the diversions of our nobility and gentry, I had mentioned gaming. He desired to know at what age this entertainment was usually taken up, and when it was laid down. How much of their time it employed; whether it ever went so high as to affect their fortunes. Whether mean vicious people, by their dexterity in that art, might not arrive at great riches, and sometimes keep our very nobles in dependance, as well as habituate them to vile companions; wholly take them from the improvement of their minds, and force them by the losses they received, to learn and practice that infamous dexterity upon others.

He was perfectly astonished with the historical account I gave him of our affairs during the last century; protesting it was only an heap of conspiracies, rebellions, murders, massacres, revolutions, banishments; the very worst effects that avarice, faction, hypocrisy, perfidiousness, cruelty, rage, madness, hatred, envy, lust, malice and ambition could produce.

His majesty in another audience, was at the pains to recapitulate the sum of all I had spoken; compared the questions he made, with the answers I had given; then taking me into his hands, and stroking me gently, delivered himself in these words, which I shall never forget, nor the manner he spoke them in. My little friend Grildrig; you have made a most admirable panegyric upon your country. You have clearly proved that ignorance, idleness, and vice are the proper ingredients for qualifying a legislator. That laws are best explained, interpreted, and applied by those whole interest and abilities lie in perverting, confounding, and eluding them. I observe among you some lines of an institution, which in its original might have been tolerable; but these half erased, and the rest wholly blurred and blotted by corruptions. It doth not appear from all you have said, how any one perfection is required towards

prejudicial: dangerous
tyranny: cruel
allowed to keep . . . as cordials: have dangerous opinions but not to spread them around
vicious: immoral
habituate them: get them used to
faction: political splits
perfidiousness: treachery
recapitulate: repeat
panegyric: speech of praise
legislator: politician
eluding: avoiding
an institution: a society

COMMENTARY
The king believes that people should be entitled to their own opinions and that they should not state them if they cause a public disturbance. He wonders if the upper classes' habit of gambling leads them into debt and crime and so prevents them from carrying out their duties. He thinks that England's history appears to be full of conflict and hate.

the procurement of any one station among you; much less that men are ennobled on account of their virtue, that priests are advanced for their piety or learning, soldiers for their conduct or valour, judges for their integrity, senators for the love of their country, or counsellors for their wisdom. As for yourself (continued the king) who have spent the greatest part of your life in travelling; I am well disposed to hope you may hitherto have escaped many vices of your country. But, by what I have gathered from your own relation, and the answers I have with much pains wringed and extorted from you; I cannot but conclude the bulk of your natives, to be the most pernicious race of little odious vermin that nature ever suffered to crawl upon the surface of the earth.

COMMENTARY

The king finishes stating his views on England by saying that England is in fact the most dishonest and rotten country he has heard of and he hopes that Gulliver has escaped its influence through traveling abroad.

the procurement: gaining
pernicious: destructive

7

Look out for . . .
- **the disagreement between Gulliver and the king about gunpowder. Who do you agree with?**
- **Gulliver's opinions about the Brobdingnagians' belief that simplicity is good.**

The author's love of his country. He makes a proposal of much advantage to the king, which is rejected. The king's great ignorance in politics. The learning of that country very imperfect and confined. Their laws, and military affairs, and parties in the state.

Nothing but an extreme love of truth could have hindered me from concealing this part of my story. It was in vain to discover my resentments, which were always turned into ridicule: and I was forced to rest with patience, while my noble and most beloved country was so injuriously treated. I am heartily sorry as any of my readers can possibly be, that such an occasion was given: but this prince happened to be so curious and inquisitive upon every particular, that it could not consist either with gratitude or good manners to refuse giving him what satisfaction I was able. Yet thus much I may be allowed to say in my own vindication; that I artfully eluded many of his questions; and gave to every point a more favourable turn by many degrees than the strictness of truth would allow. For, I have always born that laudable partiality to my own country, which Dionysius Halicarnassensis with so much

confined: limited
discover my resentments: voice my
   disagreement
injuriously: harmfully
laudable: admirable
Dionysius Halicarnassensis: a historical
   writer who had written favorably of
   his country

COMMENTARY
Gulliver explains to the reader that he felt it was his duty to show England in a good light and apologizes for failing.

justice recommends to an historian. I would hide the frailties and deformities of my political mother, and place her virtues and beauties in the most advantageous light. This was my sincere endeavour in those many discourses I had with that monarch, although it unfortunately failed of success.

But, great allowances should be given to a king who lives wholly secluded from the rest of the world, and must therefore be altogether unacquainted with the manners and customs that most prevail in other nations: the want of which knowledge will ever produce many *prejudices*, and a certain *narrowness of thinking*, from which we and the politer countries of Europe are wholly exempted. And it would be hard indeed, if so remote a prince's notions of virture and vice were to be offered as a standard for all mankind.

To confirm what I have now said, and further to show the miserable effects of a *confined education*, I shall here insert a passage which will hardly obtain belief. In hopes to ingratiate myself farther into his majesty's favour, I told him of an invention discovered between three and four hundred years ago, to make a certain powder, into an heap of which the smallest spark of fire falling, would kindle the whole in a moment, although it were as big as a mountain; and make it all fly up in the air together, with a noise and agitation greater than thunder. That, a proper quantity of this powder rammed into an hollow tube of brass or iron, according to its bigness, would drive a ball of iron or lead with such violence and speed, as nothing was able to sustain its force. That, the largest balls thus discharged, would not only destroy whole ranks of an army at once, but batter the strongest walls to the ground, sink down ships with a thousand men in each, to the bottom of the sea; and when linked together by a chain, would cut through masts and rigging; divide hundreds of bodies in the middle, and lay all waste before them. That we often put this powder into large hollow balls of iron, and discharged them by an engine into some city we were besieging, which would rip up the pavement, tear the houses to pieces, burst and throw splinters on every side, dashing out the brains of all who came near. That I knew the ingredients very well, which were cheap, and common; I understood the manner of compounding them and could direct his workmen

---

COMMENTARY

Gulliver tells the reader that the king's lack of contact with any other country has made him narrow-minded, which is why he does not understand England. The reader is left to decide whether they agree with the king's or Gulliver's views of England. Gulliver then offers the king the recipe for gunpowder, explaining the damage it can cause.

political mother: England
secluded from: cut off from
exempted: without
obtain belief: be believed
ingratiate: gain favor for
kindle: light
compounding: mixing

how to make those tubes of a size proportionable to all other things in his majesty's kingdom, and the largest need not be above two hundred foot long; twenty or thirty of which tubes, charged with the proper quantity of powder and balls, would batter down the walls of the strongest town in his dominions in a few hours, or destroy the whole metropolis, if ever it should pretend to dispute his absolute commands. This I humbly offered to his majesty, as a small tribute of acknowledgement in return for so many marks that I had received of his royal favour and protection.

The king was struck with horror at the description I had given of those terrible engines, and the proposal I had made. He was amazed how so impotent and grovelling an insect as I (these were his expressions) could entertain such inhuman ideas, and in so familiar a manner as to appear wholly unmoved at all the scenes of blood and desolation, which I had painted as the common effect of those destructive machines; whereof he said, some evil genius, enemy to mankind, must have been the first contriver. As for himself, he protested, that although few things delighted him so much as new discoveries in art or in nature, yet he would rather lose half his kingdom than be privy to such a secret, which he commanded me, as I valued my life, never to mention any more.

A strange effect of *narrow principles* and *short views*! that a prince possessed of every quality which procures veneration, love and esteem, of strong parts, great wisdom and profound learning; endued with admirable talents for government, and almost adored by his subjects; should from a *nice unnecessary scruple*, whereof in Europe we can have no conception, let slip an opportunity put into his hands, that would have made him absolute master of the lives, the liberties, and the fortunes of his people. Neither do I say this was the least intention to detract from the many virtues of that excellent king, whose character I am sensible will on this account be very much lessened in the opinion of an English reader: but, I take this defect among them to have risen from their ignorance, by not having hitherto reduced *politics* into a science, as the more acute wits of Europe have done. For, I remember very well, in a

tribute of acknowledgement: token of
    thanks
impotent: powerless
be privy to: share
procures veneration: gains praise
scruple: principle
sensible: aware
science: laws and rules
more acute wits: more intelligent people

COMMENTARY
The king is horrified by Gulliver's description of explosions and cannons and says that he is amazed someone so small could dream up such evil things. He refuses to have anything to do with gunpowder. Gulliver is surprised that the king wants to miss out on an invention that would give him total power over his people. Again, he thinks the king is being narrow-minded.

discourse one day with the king, when I happened to say there were several thousand books among us written upon the *art of government*, it gave him (directly contrary to my intention) a very mean opinion of our understandings. He professed both to abominate and despise all mystery, refinement, and intrigue, either in a prince or a minister. He could not tell what I meant by *secrets of state*, where an enemy or some rival nation were not in the case. He confined the knowledge of governing within very *narrow bounds;* to common sense and reason, to justice and lenity, to the speedy determination of civil and criminal causes; with some other obvious topics which are not worth considering. And, he gave it for his opinion, that whoever could make two ears of corn, or two blades of grass to grow upon a spot of ground where only one grew before; would deserve better of mankind, and do more essential service to his country, that the whole race of politicians put together.

The learning of this people is very defective, consisting only in morality, history, poetry and mathematics, wherein they must be allowed to excel. But, the last of these is wholly applied to what may be useful in life, to the improvement of agriculture and all mechanical arts; so that among us it would be little esteemed. And as to ideas, entities, abstractions and transcendentals, I could never drive the least conception into their heads.

No law of that country must exceed in words the number of letters in their alphabet, which consists only of two and twenty. But indeed, few of them extend even to that length. They are expressed in the most plain and simple terms, wherein those people are not mercurial enough to discover above one interpretation. And, to write a comment upon any law, is a capital crime. As to the decision of civil causes, or proceedings against criminals, their precedents are so few, that they have little reason to boast of any extraordinary skill in either.

They have had the art of printing, as well as the Chinese, time out of mind. But their libraries are not very large; for that of the king's which is reckoned the largest, doth not amount to above a thousand volumes, placed in a gallery of twelve hundred foot long, from when I had liberty to borrow what books I

COMMENTARY

Gulliver explains to the king that his country needs to learn the science of politics. The king, however, believes that running a country should be about common sense, reason, and fairness, rather than complicated plotting and scheming. In their studies and their laws, the Brobdingnagians also believe that simplicity and practicality are the most important things. Gulliver thinks this is a sign of weakness.

mean: low
abominate: detest
mystery: secrecy
refinement: cunning
intrigue: plotting
defective: imperfect
entities, abstractions and transcendentals: technical terms in philosophy
conception: understanding
mercurial: lively
precedents: past cases that are used to decide present ones
time out of mind: longer than can be remembered

pleased. The queen's joiner had contrived in one of Glumdalclitch's rooms a kind of wooden machine five and twenty foot high, formed like a standing ladder; the steps were each fifty foot long: it was indeed a moveable pair of stairs, the lowest end placed at ten foot distance from the wall of the chamber. The book I had a mind to read was put up leaning against the wall. I first mounted to the upper step of the ladder, and turning my face towards the book, began at the top of the page, and so walking to the right and left about eight or ten paces according to the length of the lines, till I had gotten a little below the level of mine eyes; and then descending gradually till I came to the bottom: after which I mounted again, and began the other page in the same manner, and so turned over the leaf, which I could easily do with both my hands, for it was as thick and stiff as a paste-board, and in the largest folios not above eighteen or twenty foot long.

Their style is clear, masculine, and smooth, but not florid, for they avoid nothing more than multiplying unnecessary words, or using various expressions. I have perused many of their books, especially those in history and morality. Among the latter I was much diverted with a little old treatise, which always lay in Glumdalclitch's bedchamber, and belonged to her governess, a grave elderly gentlewoman, who dealt in writings of morality and devotion. The book treats of the weakness of human kind, and is in little esteem except among women and the vulgar. However, I was curious to see what an author of that country could say upon such a subject. This writer went through all the usual topics of European moralists, showing how diminutive, contemptible, and helpless an animal was man in his own nature; how unable to defend himself from the inclemencies of the air, or the fury of wild beasts: how much he was excelled by one creature in strength, by another in speed, by a third in foresight, by a fourth in industry. He added, that nature was degenerated in these latter declining ages of the world, and could now produce only small abortive births in comparison of those in ancient times. He said it was very reasonable to think, not only that the species of men were originally much larger, but also that there must have been giants in former

COMMENTARY
The Brobdingnagians have few books because they do not believe in writing just for the sake of it. These books are written in a simple style. Gulliver has read one of Glumdalclitch's books, which is about how the human race is a weak and defenseless species that must have been greater in the past.

folios: books   *vulgar*: ordinary people
florid: flowery   *inclemencies*: storms

ages, which, as it is asserted by history and tradition, so it hath been confirmed by huge bones and skulls casually dug up in several parts of the kingdom, far exceeding the common dwindled race of man in our days. He argued, that the very laws of nature absolutely required we should have been made in the beginning, of a size more large and robust, not so liable to destruction from every little accident of a tile falling from a house, or a stone cast from the hand of a boy, or of being drowned in a little brook. From this way of reasoning the author drew several moral applications useful in the conduct of life, but needless here to repeat. For my own part, I could not avoid reflecting, how universally this talent was spread of drawing lectures in morality, or indeed rather matter of discontent and repining, from the quarrels we raise with nature. And, I believe upon a strict enquiry, those quarrels might be shown as ill-grounded among us, as they are among that people.

As to their military affairs; they boast that the king's army consists of an hundred and seventy six thousand foot, and thirty two thousand horse: if that may be called an army which is made up of tradesmen in the several cities, and farmers in the country, whose commanders are only the nobility and gentry, without pay or reward. They are indeed perfect enough in their exercises, and under very good discipline, wherein I saw no great merit; for, how should it be otherwise, where every farmer is under the command of his own landlord, and every citizen under that of the principal men in his own city, chosen after the manner of Venice by ballot?

I have often seen the militia of Lorbrulgrud drawn out to exercise in a great field near the city, of twenty miles square. They were in all not above twenty-five thousand foot, and six thousand horse; but it was impossible for me to compute their number, considering the space of ground they took up. A cavalier mounted on a large steed might be about ninety foot high. I have seen this whole body of horse upon the word of command draw their swords at once, and brandish them in the air. Imagination can figure nothing so grand, so surprising and so astonishing. It looked as if ten thousand flashes of lightning were darting at the same time from every quarter of the sky.

COMMENTARY

The writer of the book Gulliver is reading feels that humans are getting worse rather than better. Gulliver says he has read similar things in England and disagrees with them. Gulliver describes the king's army. It is not a professional one as in England but is made up of people who have other jobs and who are not paid. However, they seem to be just as disciplined. Gulliver finds their military displays a spectacular sight.

dwindled: shrunken
the very laws of nature: physical necessities
robust: strongly built
universally: widely
matter of discontent and repining: grumbling and fretting
ill-grounded: irrelevant
foot: foot soldiers
brandish: wave

I was curious to know how this prince, to whose dominions there is no access from any other country, came to think of armies, or to teach his people the practice of military discipline. But I was soon informed, both by conversation, and reading their histories. For, in the course of many ages they have been troubled with the same disease, to which the whole race of mankind is subject: the nobility often contending for power, the people for liberty, and the king for absolute dominion. All which, however happily tempered by the laws of that kingdom, have been sometimes violated by each of the three parties; and have more than once occasioned civil wars, the last whereof was happily put an end to by this prince's grandfather in a general composition; and the militia then settled with common consent hath been ever since kept in

►► the strictest duty.

REWIND: . . . the strictest duty.
Gulliver has a long discussion with the king about the differences between England and Brobdingnag. Gulliver begins by praising England, describing it as a perfect kingdom with a noble government. The king, however, doubts Gulliver's description and, after questioning him at length, decides that England is in fact full of people interested only in gaining power, influence, and money for themselves. Gulliver also proudly describes the invention of gunpowder, which he offers as a gift to the king, who is, however, horrified at such a destructive and dangerous substance. Gulliver continues by describing to the reader other aspects of Brobdingnag's culture, such as the fact that their laws are always kept simple and that their learning is always put to practical uses. Finally, he explains that even though they never meet people from other countries the king still has an army, which is used to prevent civil wars.

---

absolute dominion: total power
violated: broken
composition: agreement

COMMENTARY
The Brobdingnagians have no enemies from other countries but keep an army to prevent civil wars.

Look out for . . .
● the way in which Gulliver escapes Brobdingnag and his feelings for Glumdalclitch.
● the difficulty Gulliver has in adapting to living with people his own size.

The king and queen make a progress to the frontiers. The author attends them. The manner in which he leaves the country very particularly related. He returns to England.

I had always a strong impulse that I should some time recover my liberty, although it were impossible to conjecture by what means, or to form any project with the least hope of succeeding. The ship in which I sailed was the first ever known to be driven within sight of that coast, and the king had given strict orders that if at any time another appeared, it should be taken ashore, and with all its crew and passengers brought in a tumbril to Lorbrulgrud. He was strongly bent to get me a woman of my own size, by whom I might propagate the breed: but I think I should rather have died than undergone the disgrace of leaving a posterity to be kept in cages like tame canary birds, and perhaps in time sold about the kingdom to persons of quality for curiosities. I was indeed treated with much kindness; I was the favourite of a great king and queen, and the delight of the whole court, but it was upon such a foot as ill became the dignity of human kind. I could never forget those domestic pledges

COMMENTARY
Even though Gulliver is well treated he still wants to return home one day to be with people his own size. The king wants to find him a woman of his size so that he can breed, but Gulliver could not bear the idea of leaving children to be kept like tame animals and stared at as freaks.

progress: journey
very particularly related: told in detail
impulse: belief
tumbril: cart
was strongly bent: desired
a posterity: children
domestic pledges: family duties

I had left behind me. I wanted to be among people with whom I could converse upon even terms, and walk about the streets and fields without fear of being trod to death like a frog or young puppy. But, my deliverance came sooner than I expected, and in a manner not very common: the whole story and circumstances of which I shall faithfully relate.

I had now been two years in this country; and about the beginning of the third, Glumdalclitch and I attended the king and queen in progress to the south coast of the kingdom. I was carried as usual in my travelling-box, which, as I have already described, was a very convenient closet of twelve foot wide. I had ordered a hammock to be fixed by silken ropes from the four corners at the top: to break the jolts, when a servant carried me before him on horseback, as I sometimes desired, and would often sleep in my hammock while we were upon the road. On the roof of my closet, set not directly over the middle of the hammock, I ordered the joiner to cut out a hole of a foot square to give me air in hot weather as I slept, which hole I shut at pleasure with a board that drew backwards and forwards through a groove.

When we came to our journey's end, the king thought proper to pass a few days at a palace he hath near Flanflasnic, a city within eighteen English miles of the seaside. Glumdalclitch and I were much fatigued; I had gotten a small cold, but the poor girl was so ill as to be confined to her chamber. I longed to see the ocean, which must be the only scene of my escape, if ever it should happen. I pretended to be worse that I really was, and desired leave to take the fresh air of the sea, with a page whom I was very fond of, and who had sometimes been trusted with me. I shall never forget with what unwillingness Glumdalclitch consented, nor the strict charge she gave the page to be careful of me, bursting at the same time into a flood of tears, as if she had some foreboding of what was to happen. The boy took me out in my box about half an hour's walk from the palace, towards the rocks on the seashore. I ordered him to set me down, and lifting up one of my sashes, cast many a wistful melancholy look towards the sea. I found myself not very well, and told the page that I had a mind to take a nap in my hammock, which I hoped would

deliverance: escape
much fatigued: exhausted
foreboding: omen

COMMENTARY
Gulliver describes how one day he was with the king and queen on a journey to the coast. He still travels in his box, which is more comfortable than ever. At the coast, he pretends that he is feeling ill and asks Glumdalclitch if he can be taken to the sea to get fresh air. He is taken there by a servant boy who leaves him in his box to sleep.

do me good. I got in, and the boy shut the window close down, to keep out the cold. I soon fell asleep: and all I can conjecture is, that while I slept, the page, thinking no danger could happen, went among the rocks to look for birds eggs; having before observed him from my window searching about, and picking up one or two in the clefts. Be that as it will, I found myself suddenly awaked with a violent pull upon the ring which was fastened at the top of my box, for the conveniency of carriage. I felt the box raised very high in the air, and then born forward with prodigious speed. The first jolt had like to have shaken me out of my hammock; but afterwards the motion was easy enough. I called out several times as loud as I could raise my voice, but all to no purpose. I looked towards my windows, and could see nothing but the clouds and sky. I heard a noise just over my head like the clapping of wings; and then began to perceive the woeful condition I was in; that some eagle had got the ring of my box in his beak, with an intent to let it fall on a rock, like a tortoise in a shell, and then pick out my body and devour it. For the sagacity and smell of this bird enable him to discover his quarry at a great distance, although better concealed than I could be within a two inch board.

COMMENTARY

Gulliver is awakened by a violent jolt, and he is carried up into the air by an eagle that has seen his box and wants to eat Gulliver.

clefts: gaps in the rocks
woeful condition: awful position
sagacity: exceptional intelligence

In a little time I observed the noise and flutter of wings to increase very fast, and my box was tossed up and down like a signpost in a windy day. I heard several bangs or buffets, as I though, given to the eagle (for such I am certain it must have been that held the ring of my box in his beak) and then all on a sudden felt myself falling perpendicularly down for above a minute; but with such incredible swiftness that I almost lost my breath. My fall was stopped by a terrible squash, that sounded louder to mine ears than the cataract of Niagara; after which I was quite in the dark for another minute, and then my box began to rise so high that I could see light from the tops of my windows. I now perceived that I was fallen into the sea. My box, by the weight of my body, the goods that were in, and the broad plates of iron fixed for strength at the four corners of the top and bottom, floated about five foot deep in water. I did then, and do now suppose, that the eagle which flew away with my box was pursued by two or three others, and forced to let me drop while he was defending himself against the rest, who hoped to share in the prey. The plates of iron fastened at the bottom of the box (for those were the strongest), preserved the balance while it fell; and hindered it from being broken on the surface of the water. Every joint of it was well grooved, and the door did not move on hinges; but up and down like a sash; which kept my closet so tight that very little water came in. I got with much difficulty out of my hammock, having first ventured to draw back the slip board on the roof already mentioned, contrived on purpose to let in air, for want of which I found myself almost stifled.

How often did I then wish myself with my dear Glumdalclitch, from whom one single hour had so far divided me! And I may say with truth, that in the midst of my own misfortune, I could not forbear lamenting my poor nurse, the grief she would suffer for my loss, the displeasure of the queen and the ruin of her fortune. Perhaps many travellers have not been under greater difficulties and distress than I was at this juncture, expecting every moment to see my box dashed in pieces, or at least overset by the first violent blast, or a rising wave. A breach in one single pane of glass would have been immediate death: nor

---

perpendicularly: vertically
cataract of Niagara: Niagara Falls
stifled: suffocated
breach: gap

COMMENTARY
The eagle is attacked by other birds and Gulliver falls into the sea where he floats in five feet of water. He regrets the misery Glumdalclitch will feel at having lost him. He also worries she will get into trouble for losing him.

could any thing have preserved the windows but the strong lattice wires placed on the outside against accidents in travelling. I saw the water ooze in at several crannies, although the leaks were not considerable; and I endeavoured to stop them as well as I could. I was not able to lift up the roof of my closet, which otherwise I certainly should have done, and sat on the top of it, where I might at least preserve myself from being shut up, as I may call it, in the hold. Or, if I escaped these dangers for a day or two, what could I expect but a miserable death of cold and hunger! I was four hours under these circumstances, expecting and indeed wishing every moment to be my last.

I have already told the reader, that there were two strong staples fixed upon the side of my box which had no window, and into which the servant, who used to carry me on horseback, would put a leathern belt, and buckle it about his waist. Being in this disconsolate state, I heard, or at least thought I heard some kind of grating noise on that side of my box where the staples were fixed; and soon after I began to fancy that the box was pulled, or towed along in the sea; for I now and then felt a sort of tugging, which made the waves rise near the tops of my windows, leaving me almost in the dark. This gave me some faint hopes of relief, although I were not able to imagine how it could be brought about. I ventured to unscrew one of my chairs, which were always fastened to the floor; and having made a hard shift to screw it down again directly under the slipping-board that I had lately opened; I mounted on the

COMMENTARY
Gulliver feels that he will soon die through drowning, suffocation, or hunger. Then he hears a noise and can feel his box being towed along by something.

lattice: crisscross
disconsolate: depressed

chair, and putting my mouth as near as I could to the hole, I called for help in a loud voice, and in all the languages I understood. I then fastened my handkerchief to a stick I usually carried, and thrusting it up the hole, waved it several times in the air; that if any boat or ship were near, the seamen might conjecture some unhappy mortal to be shut up in the box.

I found no effect from all I could do, but plainly perceived my closet to be moved along; and in the space of an hour, or better, that side of the box where the staples were, and had no window, struck against something that was hard. I apprehended it to be a rock, and found myself tossed more than ever. I plainly heard a noise upon the cover of my closet, like that of a cable, and the grating of it as it passed through the ring. I then found myself hoisted up by degrees at least three foot higher than I was before. Whereupon, I again thrust up my stick and handkerchief, calling for help till I was almost hoarse. In return to which, I heard a great shout repeated three times, giving me such transports of joy as are not to be conceived but by those who feel them. I now heard a trampling over my head; and somebody calling through the hole with a loud voice in the English tongue: *if there be anybody below, let them speak.* I answered, I was an Englishman, drawn by ill fortune into the greatest calamity that ever any creature underwent; and begged, by all that was moving, to be delivered out of the dungeon I was in. The voice replied, I was safe, for my box was fastened to their ship; and the carpenter should immediately come, and saw an hole in the cover, large enough to pull me out. I answered, that was needless, and would take too much time; for there was no more to be done, but let one of the crew put his finger into the ring, and take the box out of the sea into the ship, and so into the captain's cabin. Some of them upon hearing me talk so wildly, thought I was mad; others laughed; for indeed it never came into my head, that I was not got among people of my own stature and strength. The carpenter came, and in a few minutes sawed a passage about four foot square; then let down a small ladder, upon which I mounted, and from thence was taken into the ship in a very weak condition.

transports of joy: overwhelming happiness
calamity: disaster

COMMENTARY
Gulliver opens his roof and calls out, waving his handkerchief. He hears English voices calling out from the ship that is pulling him along. He replies, thinking that they are giants who could just lift his box out of the water.

The sailors were all in amazement, and asked me a thousand questions, which I had no inclination to answer. I was equally confounded at the sight of so many pygmies; for such I took them to be, after having so long accustomed mine eyes to the monstrous objects I had left. But the captain, Mr Thomas Wilcocks, an honest worthy Shropshire man, observing I was ready to faint, took me into his cabbin, gave me a cordial to comfort me, and made me turn in upon his own bed; advising me to take a little rest, of which I had great need. Before I went to sleep I gave him to understand, that I had some valuable furniture in my box too good to be lost; a fine hammock, an handsome field-bed, two chairs, a table and a cabinet: that my closet was hung on all sides, or rather quilted with silk and cotton: that if he would let one of the crew bring my closet into his cabin, I would open it before him and show him my goods. The captain hearing me utter these absurdities, concluded I was raving: however (I suppose to pacify me), he promised to give order as I desired; and going upon deck, sent some of his men down into my closet, from whence (as I afterwards found) they drew up all my goods, and stripped off

cordial: drink

COMMENTARY
When he is taken on board the ship, Gulliver sees the sailors and thinks that they look like Lilliputians because he is unused to seeing people his own size. The captain listens to Gulliver's description of his box and thinks he is mad.

the quilting; but the chairs, cabinet and bedstead being screwed to the floor, were much damaged by the ignorance of the seamen, who tore them up by force. Then they knocked off some of the boards for the use of the ship; and when they had got all they had a mind for, let the hulk drop into the sea, which by reason of many breaches made in the bottom and sides, sunk to rights. And indeed I was glad not to have been a spectator of the havock they made; because I am confident it would have sensibly touched me by bringing former passages into my mind, which I had rather forget.

I slept some hours, but perpetually disturbed with dreams of the place I had left, and the dangers I had escaped. However, upon waking I found myself much recovered. It was now about eight o'clock at night, and the captain ordered supper immediately, thinking I had already fasted too long. He entertained me with great kindness, observing me not to look wildly, or talk inconsistently, and when we were left alone, desired I would give him a relation of my travels, and by what accident I came to be set adrift in that monstrous wooden chest. He said, that about twelve o'clock at noon, as he was looking through his glass, he spied it at a distance, and thought it was sail, which he had a mind to make; being not much out of course, in hopes of buying some biscuit, his own beginning to fall short. That, upon coming nearer, and finding his error, he sent out his long-boat to discover what I was; that his men came back in a fright, swearing they had seen a swimming house. That he laughed at their folly, and went himself in the boat, ordering his men to take a strong cable along with them. That the weather being calm, he rowed round me several times, observed my windows, and the wire lattices that defend them. That he discovered two staples upon one side, which was all of boards, without any passage of light. He then commanded his men to row up to that side; and fastning a cable to one of the staples, ordered his men to tow my chest (as he called it) towards the ship. When it was there, he gave directions to fasten another cable to the ring fixed in the cover, and to raise up my chest with pullies, which all the sailors were not able to do above two or three foot. He said, they saw my stick and handkerchief thrust out of the hole, and

---

to rights: completely
sensibly touched me: moved me
passages: experiences
inconsistently: in a confused way

COMMENTARY
The crew strip Gulliver's box of anything they think is useful and then drop it into the sea. After Gulliver has had a long sleep, the captain of the ship explains the way in which he was rescued.

concluded, that some unhappy man must be shut up in the cavity. I asked whether he or the crew had seen any prodigious birds in the air about the time he first discovered me: to which he answered, that discoursing this matter with the sailors while I was asleep, one of them said he had observed three eagles flying towards the north; but remarked nothing of their being larger than the usual size; which I suppose must be imputed to the great height they were at: and he could not guess the reason of my question. I then asked the captain how far he reckoned we might be from land; he said, by the best computation he could make, we were at least an hundred leagues. I assured him, that he must be mistaken by almost half, for I had not left the country from whence I came above two hours before I dropped into the sea. Whereupon he began again to think that my brain was disturbed, of which he gave me a hint, and advised me to go to bed in a cabin he had provided. I assured him I was well refreshed with his good entertainment and company, and as much in my senses as ever I was in my life. He then grew serious, and desired to ask me freely whether I were not troubled in mind by the consciousness of some enormous crime, for which I was punished at the command of some prince, by exposing me in that chest; as great criminals in other countries have been forced to sea in a leaky vessel without provisions: for, although he should be sorry to have taken so ill a man into his ship, yet he would engage his word to set me safe on shore in the first port where we arrived. He added, that his suspicions were much increased by some very absurd speeches I had delivered at first to the sailors, and afterwards to himself, in relation to my closet or chest, as well as by my odd looks and behaviour while I was at supper.

I begged his patience to hear me tell my story; which I faithfully did from the last time I left England, to the moment he first discovered me. And, as truth always forceth its way into rational minds; so, this honest worthy gentleman, who had some tincture of learning, and very good sense, was immediately convinced of my candour and veracity. But, further to confirm all I had said, I entreated him to give order that my cabinet should be brought, of which I kept the key in my pocket (for he had already informed me of how the

COMMENTARY

Gulliver disagrees with the captain about how near land they are. Because Gulliver is behaving oddly the captain thinks he is mad and wonders if Gulliver was locked in his box as a punishment for a dreadful crime.

discoursing: discussing
imputed to: explained by
tincture: trace
veracity: honesty

seamen disposed of my closet); I opened it in his presence, and showed him the small collection of rarities I made in the country from which I had been so strangely delivered. There was the comb I had contrived out of the stumps of the king's beard; and another of the same materials, but fixed into a paring of her majesty's thumb-nail, which served for the back. There was a collection of needles and pins from a foot to a half a yard long. Four wasp-stings, like joiners' tacks: some combings of the queen's hair: a gold ring which one day she made me a present of in a most obliging manner, taking it from her little finger, and throwing it over my head like a collar. I desired the captain would please to accept this ring in return of his civilities; which he absolutely refused. I showed him a corn that I had cut off with my own hand from a maid of honour's toe; it was about the bigness of a Kentish pippin, and grown so hard, that when I returned to England, I got it hollowed into a cup and set in silver. Lastly, I desired him to see the breeches I had then on, which were made of a mouse's skin.

I could force nothing on him but a footman's tooth, which I observed him to examine with great curiosity, and found he had a fancy for it. He received it with abundance of thanks, more than such a trifle could deserve. It was drawn by an unskilful surgeon in a mistake from one of Glumdalclitch's men, who was afflicted with the toothache; but it was as sound as any in his head. I got it cleaned, and put it into my cabinet. It was about a foot long, and four inches in diameter.

The captain was well satisfied with this plain relation I had given him; and said, he hoped when we returned to England, I would oblige the world by putting it in paper, and making it public. My answer was that I thought we were already over-stocked with books of travels: that nothing could now pass which was not extraordinary; wherein I doubted, some authors less consulted truth than their own vanity or interest, or the diversion of ignorant readers. That my story would contain little besides common events, without those ornamental descriptions of strange plants, trees, birds, and other animals; or the barbarous customs and idolatry of savage people, with which most writers

---

COMMENTARY

Gulliver explains his story to the captain and shows him some of the things he had stored in the box. The captain begins to believe him and eventually accepts the gift of a giant tooth, which Gulliver had got from one of the servants at court. The captain tells Gulliver that he should write down an account of his travels. Gulliver says that there is too much travel writing around already in which the writers exaggerate their experiences. He says that his travels would appear as ordinary compared to theirs.

---

paring: cutting
Kentish pippin: an apple
footman: servant

abundance of: much
sound: good, healthy
barbarous: primitive

abound. However, I thanked him for his good opinion, and promised to take the matter into my thoughts.

He said he wondered at one thing very much, which was, to hear me speak so loud, asking me whether the king or queen of that country were thick of hearing. I told him it was what I had been used to for above two years past; and that I admired as much at the voices of him and his men, who seemed to me only to whisper, and yet I could hear them well enough. But, when I spoke in that country, it was like a man talking in the street to another looking out from the top of a steeple, unless when I was placed on a table, or held in any person's hand. I told him, I had likewise observed another thing; that when I first got into the ship, and the sailors stood all about me, I thought they were the most little contemptible creatures I had ever beheld. For, indeed, while I was in that prince's country, I could never endure to look in a glass after mine eyes had been accustomed to such prodigious objects; because the comparison gave me so despicable a conceit of myself. The captain said, that while we were at supper, he observed me to look at everything with a sort of wonder; and that I often seemed hardly able to contain my laughter; which he knew not well how to take, but imputed it to some disorder in my brain. I answered, it was very true; and I wondered how I could forbear, when I saw his dishes of the size of a silver threepence, a leg of pork hardly a mouthful, a cup not so big as a nutshell: and so I went on, describing the rest of his household-stuff and provisions after the same manner. For although the queen had ordered a little equipage of all things necessary for me while I was in her service, yet my ideas were wholly taken up with what I saw on every side of me, and I winked at my own littleness, as people do at their own faults. The captain understood my raillery very well, and merrily replied with the old English proverb, that he doubted mine eyes were bigger than my belly; for he did not observe my stomach so good, although I had fasted all day: and continuing in his mirth, protested he would have gladly given an hundred pounds to have seen my closet in the eagle's bill, and afterwards in its fall from so great an height into the sea; which would certainly have been a most astonishing object, worthy to

COMMENTARY

The captain asks why Gulliver always shouts. He replies that it is due to having to shout to be heard by the giants. Gulliver also says that he thought that the crew spoke in whispers. He feels that normal humans look small and pathetic. He explains that, like most humans, he is used to looking at other people's habits and faults rather than his own. This is why he feels everyone on board looks pathetic except himself.

thick of hearing: hard of hearing
glass: mirror
conceit: idea
winked at: ignored
raillery: witty criticisms

have the description of it transmitted to future ages: and the comparison of Phaethon was so obvious, that he could not forbear applying it, although I did not much admire the conceit.

The captain having been at Tonquin, was in his return to England driven north-eastward to the latitude of 44 degrees, and of longitude 143. But meeting a trade wind two days after I came on board him, we sailed southward a long time, and coasting New Holland, kept our course west-south-west, and the south-south-west till we doubled the Cape of Good Hope. Our voyage was very prosperous, but I shall not trouble the reader with a journal of it. The captain called in at one or two ports, and sent in his long-boat for provisions and fresh water, but I never went out of the ship till we came into the Downs, which was on the 3rd day of June 1706, about nine months after my escape. I offered to leave my goods in security for payment of my freight; but the captain protested he would not receive one farthing. We took kind leave of each other; and I made him promise he would come to see me at my house in Redriff. I hired a horse and guide for five shillings, which I borrowed of the captain.

As I was on the road, observing the littleness of the houses, the trees, the cattle and the people, I began to think myself in Lilliput. I was afraid of trampling on every traveller I met, and often called aloud to have them stand out of the way, so that I had like to have gotten one or two broken heads for my impertinence.

When I came to my own house, for which I was forced to enquire, one of the servants opening the door, I bent down to go in (like a goose under a gate) for fear of striking my head. My wife ran out to embrace me, but I stooped lower than her knees, thinking she could otherwise never be able to reach my mouth. My daughter kneeled to ask my blessing, but I could not see her till she arose; having been so long used to stand with my head and eyes erect to above sixty foot; and then I went to take her up with one hand, by the waist. I looked down upon the servants, and one of two friends who were in the house, as if they had been pygmies, and I a giant. I told my wife she had been too

---

transmitted: passed on

Phaethon: the son of the Greek sun god who almost set fire to the earth by driving his chariot too close to it. He was eventually struck down by Zeus, the king of the gods.

Tonquin: a port in North Vietnam

New Holland: Australia

impertinence: rudeness

COMMENTARY

The journey back home is described. When Gulliver lands in England, he feels he is in Lilliput because everything looks so small. He is so used to dealing with giants that he behaves in a strange way when he meets his family.

thrifty, for I found she had starved herself and her daughter to nothing. In short, I behaved myself so unaccountably, that they were all of the captain's opinion when he first saw me, and concluded I had lost my wits. This I mention as an instance of the great power of habit and prejudice.

In a little time I and my family and friends came to a right understanding: but my wife protested I should never go to sea any more; although my evil destiny so ordered, that she had not power to hinder me, as the reader may know hereafter. In the meantime, I here conclude the second part of my unfortunate voyages.

THE END OF THE SECOND PART

COMMENTARY

Gulliver tells us that it is very difficult to stop thinking and behaving in certain ways once they have become habits. He finishes by telling us that his adventures have not put him off from traveling.

thrifty: careful with money
unaccountably: oddly
right understanding: understand one another
evil destiny: dreadful fate

Study guide

BEFORE READING THE BOOK

1. This first activity can be done individually or in a group. Find a large sheet of paper and divide it into two columns. At the top of the left-hand column write "Lilliput" and at the top of the right-hand column write "Brobdingnag." As you read the book, make notes about each of these places: This will help you to make comparisons between them when you have finished reading. It may be helpful to divide each column into sections with the following headings:
   - events
   - characters
   - Gulliver's character and feelings
   - places
   - ideas/themes
   - summary of good points
   - summary of bad points

LILLIPUT

Chapter 1

2. At the beginning of this chapter, Gulliver describes what happened in his life before going on his travels. This type of writing is called "autobiographical." Try to write your own autobiography up to this moment. Write a maximum of two pages. The skill is in trying to include all the important events in your life while keeping it brief and entertaining.

3. Gulliver is shipwrecked and loses all his friends. Imagine that you are in a similar position and write about the shipwreck, what happens to you, and what your feelings are. Your story could have a happy or sad ending!

4. Imagine that you are one of the Lilliputians who discovers Gulliver. Write an informal letter to a friend explaining how you felt when you found him. Describe how Gulliver appears, how he was tied down, and what happened when he woke up.

5. Imagine that you are one of the important Lilliputian officials who was in charge of bringing Gulliver into the city. Write a formal report for the emperor telling him what you did and making proposals about what you think should be done with this giant. Remember to use formal language and try to be as imaginative as possible in your suggestions about how Gulliver could be useful to the emperor.

Chapter 2

6. Imagine that you are one of the Lilliputians who has visited the town to see the giant Gulliver. You saw him pretend he was about to eat people who had fired arrows at him. Write the conversation between you and your husband or wife when you return home. Remember to describe your feelings on first seeing Gulliver and how you felt when you thought he was about to eat some people. You should also include your thoughts about

Gulliver showing mercy to them. You might find it helpful to write the conversation as a script. It could begin something like this:

Mr. Slingsel: I'm home! You won't believe the day I've just had!
Mrs. Slingsel: Tell me about him! Is he as enormous and frightening as everybody says? I'm glad they keep him chained up!

7. When Jonathan Swift wrote *Gulliver's Travels,* he invented a nonsense language for the Lilliputians to speak. However, it is quite difficult to invent a new language that sounds as if it means something even though it is totally made up. Try to write a short passage using a language you have invented. You will need to think particularly of nouns (names of things or ideas), verbs (words that describe what someone is doing), and adjectives (describing words). Include an English translation with your passage!

8. In this chapter, the Lilliputians go through Gulliver's pockets and try to describe things that they have never seen before. Imagine Gulliver was stranded on Lilliput today with a lot of the objects we take for granted. How would the Lilliputians describe them? For example, imagine you are a Lilliputian and you see a personal stereo for the first time. How would you describe what it looks like, how it works, and what noise it makes? When you have chosen your objects, write down your descriptions and then read them to a friend to see if he or she can guess what you are describing. To give you more choice, you could pretend that Gulliver has come ashore on a small boat. What sort of things would be in there?

Chapter 3

9. In this chapter, Gulliver describes the ridiculous ways in which the Lilliputians gain promotion at court. Think about the things that you are expected to do to please people, such as teachers, your parents, other adults, other teenagers, etc. Do you feel that some of these things are silly, embarrassing, or unfair? Either write an article for a magazine complaining about these things or write a short story about an occasion when someone is forced to behave in a certain way just to make someone else feel important. This could be based on your own experiences or made up.

10. At the end of the chapter, Gulliver is given a set of rules that he has to obey if he is going to be unchained. Gulliver feels that some of these are unfair. Do you agree? If you were a Lilliputian what rules would you have made before Gulliver's release from the chains?

Chapter 4

11. In this chapter, Gulliver visits the capital city, Mildendo. Design a poster that could have been put up around the city before Gulliver's arrival. It should tell people what to expect and what they should do to avoid being trodden on. It could also include a description of the "Man-Mountain" and a picture of him.

12. In the second half of this chapter, we hear about the silly arguments between the political parties in Lilliput and between Lilliput and Blefuscu. What started as minor arguments have been blown up out of all

proportion. Think about occasions when you have seen this happen between two people or within a group of people. Describe what started the arguments, how they got worse, and what happened in the end. What advice would you have given these people in order to prevent things from getting worse?

Chapter 5

13. Imagine that you are one of the Blefuscudian sailors. You keep a diary in which you describe the day when Gulliver stole your country's fleet. Remember, before that day you had no idea that such a huge person could exist. Describe how you felt when you first saw Gulliver and how you responded to what he did to the fleet. How did the people around you react?

14. In the middle of the chapter, Gulliver is made a Nardac. Based on your own knowledge of ceremonies, describe the ceremony at which you (Gulliver) are made a Nardac. Remember the language will be very formal and "flowery" (see page 38). You should also invent some of the movements and actions that are part of the ceremony. These can be as serious or silly as you like!

15. Write two news reports that describe the capture of the Blefuscudian fleet. One should be for a Blefuscudian newspaper and one for a Lilliputian newspaper. Remember that each report will describe what happened according to the writer's own point of view and will be biased toward his or her own country. Think carefully about using eye-catching headlines and dramatic, emotional language. You could draw or cut out dramatic pictures to go with the story.

Chapter 6

16. In this chapter, Gulliver describes the Lilliputian culture and way of life. Imagine that you are a Lilliputian visiting England today. What would you think of it as a place to live? Like Gulliver, you are writing down what you see so that you can explain it to the people in your own country. You will need to compare it to Lilliputian society and say whether you think England is better or worse as a place to live. You could describe some of the following:
    ● the royal family and politicians
    ● celebrities such as pop stars, film stars, and football players
    ● education
    ● food and drink
    ● sport and other leisure activities
    ● festivals and important annual events
    ● relationships between different groups of people, e.g., adults and teenagers, men and women, rich and poor, different races
    ● whether England is a good place to live in or not
    Remember, you have never seen a country like this so you may find a lot of things odd, confusing, or silly.

Chapter 7

17. In this chapter, Gulliver describes the way that jealous people plotted against him even though he had done a lot of things to help the country. On page 68 we learn who the main plotters are and some of their reasons for disliking Gulliver, and on pages 69 and 70 we hear of the charges they have brought against Gulliver. Using this information, write a short story entitled "The Plot," which describes a secret meeting held by all those who have a grudge against Gulliver. Describe where the meeting happens, the people who take part, and their reasons for wanting to get rid of Gulliver. Remember, most of them are jealous of Gulliver for various reasons.

18. Imagine that Gulliver has been put on trial by the Lilliputians. Write the speech that Gulliver would have made in his defense and the speech Flimnap would have made against him. How do they make the same actions look either very bad or very good? Remember that the language in a law court is very formal while still trying to encourage emotions in the jury.

Chapter 8

19. Imagine that you are the Lilliputian emperor and you have discovered that Gulliver, your secret weapon, has escaped and is with your enemy. You have a meeting with your ministers to discuss ways in which you could capture Gulliver. Write the minutes of the meeting, including as many imaginative ways of capturing Gulliver as possible. You could start like this:

    Minutes of meeting held on Climdlop 18, 3654 in the king's chambers. The emperor spoke about the only item on the agenda: the escape of the treacherous Man-Mountain to the dreaded enemy, Blefuscu. He asked for suggestions as to how the traitor could be recaptured. Flimnap suggested that some of the ships won in the victory over Blefuscu could sail over at night, equipped with several large, hot pokers . . .

20. When Gulliver returns home, he puts his tiny Lilliputian cows and sheep on show. Design a poster advertising the shows. You will need a catchy slogan and some details that will make people interested in coming to see the animals. You could also include newspaper reviews about the shows.

BROBDINGNAG

Chapter 1

21. Imagine that you are the captain of the *Adventure* and you are filling out your logbook at the end of the day in which you abandoned Gulliver on Brobdingnag. You will need to explain why you were off course and what happened after you anchored near shore, including your feelings on seeing the giant chasing your crew members in the boat. You should also try to explain why you left Gulliver behind. How do you feel about this?

22. Write the conversation held between the farmer and his workers just after Gulliver has been discovered. What do they think they have found and what do they suggest should be done with Gulliver? Do their views change at all when they see Gulliver is like a small man? How does the farmer respond to being offered the tiny coins?

23. Imagine that you are the farmer's wife chatting with your neighbor at the end of the first day with Gulliver. Remember that you thought he was like a disgusting insect at first but grew to be fond of him. You should describe the events of the day from the point of view of a giant looking at a midget. What does the neighbor think? How much of it does she believe?

Chapter 2

24. Imagine that you are Glumdalclitch and that you are writing your diary at the end of your first day looking after Gulliver. What do you think of him? How much do you enjoy your job? Is he just like a doll or is he better in some ways? What is he like to teach? You could describe one of the lessons. (Remember when you are writing that Glumdalclitch is only nine years old.)

25. The farmer asks the town crier to advertise the show Gulliver is to put on. Write the speech for him. Remember, you need to make the show sound like the most amazing thing on earth. To help you, think about how trailers for films describe some of the best moments of the show.

26. Imagine that you and a friend discovered a tiny human being like Gulliver today. Would you put him in a show to make money? Would you be concerned about his feelings as you showed him off as a freak? Write down the conversation you would have with your friend, imagining that one of you is in favor of making money out of Gulliver, the other feels that he should be free to do as he chooses.

Chapter 3

27. Look at the language Gulliver uses on page 108. This is the way in which the people of Brobdingnag speak to royalty. Imagine that you were going to see the king to ask for a favor. Obviously you want to please him so you praise him very highly and call him grand names. Write your speech, using the same type of language as Gulliver but inventing your own names.

28. Look at the description of Gulliver's box on page 111. Draw a detailed plan of it, including all the furniture. If possible, draw Gulliver in the room and draw something next to the box to show its size compared to the giants—perhaps a finger or face.

29. The queen's dwarf is very jealous of Gulliver and feels he may lose his job. Imagine that you are the dwarf and that you are talking to one of the palace servants who is a friend of yours. Describe your feelings on seeing Gulliver for the first time. What might happen to you now that Gulliver is in court? What are your plans for getting rid of him?

Chapter 4

30. In this chapter, Gulliver visits Brobdingnag's capital city. Imagine a Brobdingnagian comes to visit your town. Write the description he or she would put into a book to be sold back in Brobdingnag. For example, how would your houses, shops, main buildings, churches, pubs, schools, and leisure facilities be described by a giant?

Chapter 5

31. In this chapter, Gulliver describes a number of accidents and adventures that happen because of his size. Write the story "A Day in Brobdingnag" in which you (Gulliver) describe a series of things that happened to you in Brobdingnag. Try to be imaginative in coming up with your own ideas for accidents and problems that could happen. Remember, you will need to be clear about exactly how much bigger everything is in Brobdingnag.

Chapter 6

32. At the beginning of this chapter, Gulliver describes how he made chairs, a comb, and a purse out of the king's and queen's hair. Draw and label other things that Gulliver could have made using giant hair and stubble. You could also think about how he could have used such things as nail clippings, eyelashes, and extracted teeth to make gifts for the king and queen. Additionally, you could design things for Gulliver to use out of other giant waste items like empty bottles, used pens, pencil shavings, etc.

33. Gulliver cleverly invents a way of playing a spinet. Try to invent ways for Gulliver to play other musical instruments, such as a guitar, a trumpet, or a set of drums, which are twelve times larger than usual. Write down your explanations and draw pictures to help make them clear.

Chapter 7

34. Chapters 6 and 7 are all about what kind of place England is, how it is organized, and the rules that people live by. Imagine that you were in the position to take a group of people to a faraway place, which has no inhabitants to start up a new country. Describe the kind of country you would like to create, a country that you feel would be an improvement on England. You could think about the following things:
    ● Who would run the country?
    ● How would laws be made?
    ● What kind of laws would be made?
    ● Who would make sure laws were kept and what punishments would there be if they were broken?
    ● How would people be educated? What would they need to learn?
    ● How would children be brought up?

Chapter 8

35. Write another entry in Glumdalclitch's diary on the day that Gulliver is taken. What are her feelings about losing him? What does she think might have happened? Who does she blame? How does the queen react to the loss of Gulliver? Will Glumdalclitch lose her position at court?

36. Write down the conversation between the sailors on the ship that rescues Gulliver. They are talking just after he has gone to bed. What do they think of his box, which looks like a floating house? How do they respond to Gulliver's strange behavior? (Remember that Gulliver shouts a lot and thinks that the crew whisper. He also thinks they look pathetically small.) What ideas do they come up with to explain Gulliver's situation?

37. Imagine that you are one of Gulliver's children. Write a letter to a friend describing how your father behaved when he returned from his journey. How are you and the rest of the family coping with his strange behavior? Do you believe what your father tells you about his travels?

AFTER READING THE BOOK

38. While you have been reading the book you should have been filling out the chart that was described in Activity 1. Using this chart, write "A Guidebook to Lilliput and Brobdingnag." It could include the following:
    - maps and descriptions of the places to visit
    - the way you will be greeted on arrival
    - laws and customs of the country
    - important historical events
    - entertainment
    - the correct way to address important people
    - people who can be trusted and people to avoid
    - problems that may happen because of your size
    - suggestions for gifts to take home for friends and family
    Use illustrations and pictures from newspapers and magazines to make your guidebook attractive.

39. Imagine that Gulliver goes on another journey, is once again shipwrecked, and ends up on an island where the people are physically very different—perhaps they are wider than they are tall or they do everything backward. The country may even be ruled by a particular animal, whereas the humans are treated as a lower species. Describe Gulliver's experiences and what he learns about this country.

40. One of the main themes of this book is the idea that people sometimes hold fixed views about certain things, which can be challenged if they think about them from a different point of view. Gulliver learns a lot about his weaknesses and the failings of his country by seeing England from the point of view of other countries. Write a story in which someone is prejudiced against a person or type of person but changes after seeing things from their point of view. For example, a teenage boy might think that all old people are grumpy and boring but through a temporary job serving meals on wheels he discovers that each person he serves has an interesting character and history of their own and that many still live fulfilling lives.

41. Although we are usually on Gulliver's side during his travels, Swift does not intend us always to agree with Gulliver. Using the sheet from Activity 1 and/or your guidebook (Activity 38), find examples of times when Swift is critical of Lilliputians or Brobdingnagians and times when he is critical of England. Then write an essay entitled "Satire in *Gulliver's Travels*." In the essay you should explore the ways in which human society is presented and the ways in which Swift ridicules human failings. To help you in this, you should read the section on satire in the Introduction. Remember, the point of the book was to motivate people in England to look afresh at themselves and their country by mocking its faults and by proposing alternative ways of organizing a society.